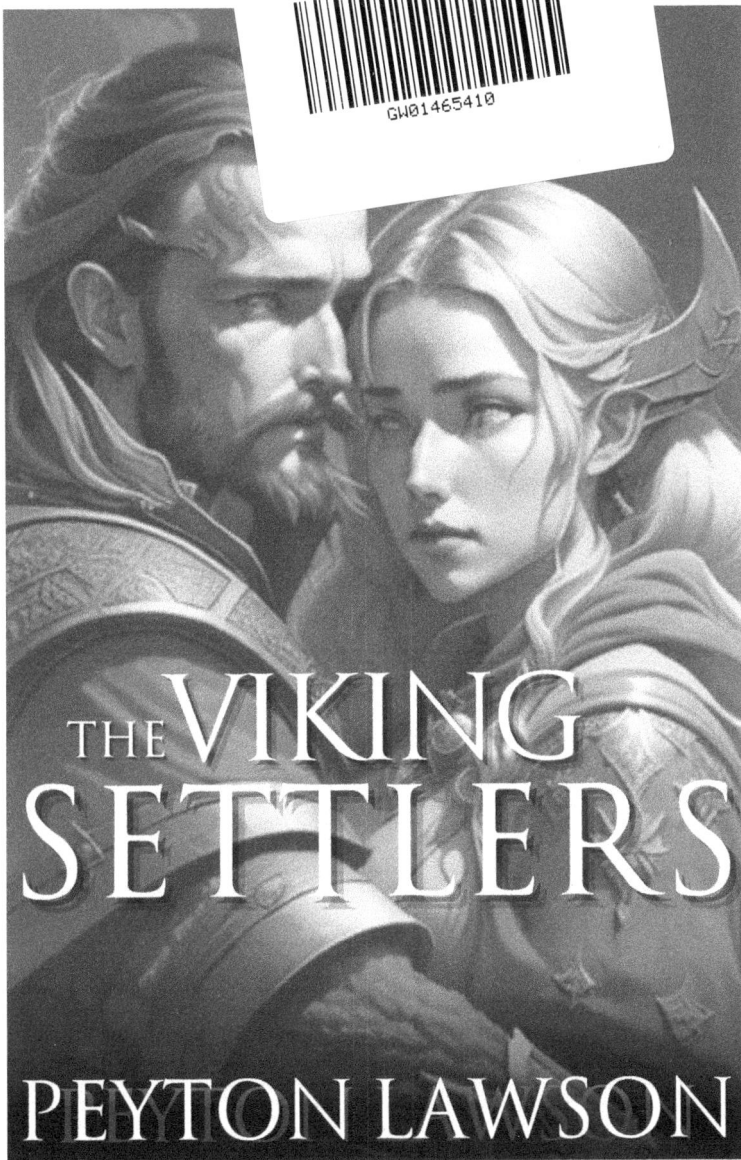

THE VIKING SETTLERS

PEYTON LAWSON

Edited by Rachael Lammie
Cover by Peyton Lawson

BEACHES AND TRAILS
PUBLISHING

ABOUT THE AUTHOR

Peyton Lawson writes Steamy Historical Viking Romance. Her edge-of-your-seat action and adventure stories feature strong, fearless characters who always get their HEA.
She enjoys reading and traveling.

For updates on book releases, book recommendations, Viking Trivia, Sales, and GIVEAWAYS, subscribe to her Newsletter!

www.peytonlawsonromance.com

GUNNAR

RESCUED BY A DANISH MAID

PROLOGUE

SVEN HAD SERVED his time as Lief's second in command and taken his reward for his service. He and his sister dreamed of sailing the seas with their families. The fulfillment of their dream left Lief without a second. The King wouldn't have that and hand-picked the perfect person for the job. At first light, Lars and his sister, Laga, had sailed to the English shores to help run the settlement at the Point.

Lars had taken to his new role as second in command like a duck to water. Lief knew the King had chosen well. Lars was young, tough, and had ample experience in fighting and serving on dangerous expeditions. For someone of his age, his skills were impressive.

Lars wanted to make the King proud. And to see how well Lief had received him and his sister, Lars wanted to make Lief proud too. While Lars appreciated Lief's continued praise and encouragement, he harboured a secret. Most of his appeared knowledge, he was faking. Lars didn't understand the technical side of running the settlement, and he wasn't too great with numbers. But his secret had stayed hidden thus far, primarily thanks to his cocky attitude and overconfidence.

Lars' skills were tested the day the King himself ventured to the Point to see how well things were going. With the help of his brothers in arms – Birgen and Olga – who travelled to the settlement with Lars, the King's tour went swimmingly.

"I have to say, young Lars, I am impressed. I knew my judgement was not misplaced," beamed the King.

"Thank you, Chieftain. Your words mean a great deal to me. Your faith in me is also appreciated," Lars bowed.

"He has proven to be an asset," Lief grinned, a sight that rarely happened.

"Glad to hear it, Lief. We have things to discuss." The King led Lief away from the group leaving Birgen, Olga, and Lars to their thoughts.

There was no avoiding it. The whispers around the settlement were that Lief believed war was on the horizon. With the stories came concerns as to who the true enemy was. Birgen and Olga had been itching to discuss it for days since their arrival, but Lars had managed to dodge their line of questioning. Now, with the King's visit, he could no longer avoid it.

"You know the Chieftain wouldn't travel from Denmark without good cause. We all know he didn't check on the Jürgensen's when they started the other settlement. Something is happening," Birgen whispered, careful not to be overheard.

"Lief believes war is coming; with this impromptu visit, I think he might be right," Olga said.

"We have always had issues with the English. They have attacked once. So, who is to say they won't try again?" Birgen asked.

"Are you scared, friend?" Lars smirked.

Birgen straightened himself up, pulling his sword and swiping it a few times in intricate formations.

"Do I look scared, brother?" Birgen laughed.

"Until we have heard the words from Lief's lips, everything is speculation. Do not concern yourself with things above your station," Lars snipped.

He hadn't meant to sound so condescending, but the truth was his gut twisted at the thought of war.

"Power is going to your head, Lars," Olga retorted. Her voice was a warning not to overstep again.

"I don't mean it like that. You know you two are like family. Speaking of family, I need to go check on Laga, see how she is settling in," Lars replied, slipping off quickly, hoping to avoid any more questions.

"Laga will be fine. She lives with her head in the clouds. I bet all this talk of war hasn't even reached her ears," Olga remarked.

Lars never could figure out why Olga disliked his sister so much. Every chance she got, she made comments about how little she thought of her or dismissed the work she did. Even if there was some feud he didn't know about, Laga was his sister, and he wouldn't have anyone talk of her in such a way.

"Laga is a competent warrior. Do not dismiss her merely because she is acting as the shepherd. I have seen her take down wolves with her bare hands. Correct me if I am wrong, Olga, but are you or are you not afraid of dogs?"

Olga stiffened and said nothing. Her face was as hard as a stone and just as unreadable.

"I thought so. Think again before you speak of my sister."

Lars hated arguing with his friends. They had given up lives of their own back in Denmark to follow him to start a new life in England. Lars believed Olga took issue with the fact that Laga was not a Viking despite her being Danish-born. Lars couldn't afford to give the dispute more thought, so he stormed through the castle in search of his sister.

As he left the castle's main gate in a blind fit, he ran straight into a tall stranger cloaked in black.

"Watch where you are going, man!" Lars barked.

"Apologies," the stranger answered, keeping his face hidden.

"Why do you seek the castle?" Lars asked, concerned.

"I seek the blacksmith."

Lars didn't think to question it further and carried on in search of Laga.

CHAPTER 1

LAGA HAD WATCHED her brother go off on adventure after adventure for as long as she could remember. She would sit at home waiting for him to return so she could hear all about the far away places, the strange customs, fashions, and eating habits of other nations. The world was so vast, and Laga wanted to see it all.

When Lars had recommended her to the King, she had been overjoyed. Travelling to these strange and mystical shores was a dream come true. She never thought of herself as anything special. She had spent her life taking care of the farm back home. These skills she discounted continuously had been her ticket to her dream, and she vowed never to disregard them again.

Some had disapproved of her because while she was Danish-born, Laga, unlike her brother Lars wasn't a Viking. However, when others leapt to criticise her, Lars was quick to defend her.

"I beg one of you to do what she does. Without her, none of you would be fed. Name anyone better at handling the livestock than Laga. Dare any of you to fight off a wolf or a bear when they come for our cattle? Do not come for my sister again. She is just as capable as any of you. Besides, her presence is on the King's orders."

Laga still remembered the smirk on her brother's face and the flash of pride in his eyes. She would never know how to thank him for this opportunity. Instead, she vowed not to have his trust misplaced. The settlement had quickly come to depend on her to tend to the flocks and herds. No one else could control the animals like her. It was almost like she could speak with them; they listened and obeyed her.

Every day, Laga ventured a little further afield while always keeping the settlement in sight. She longed to explore these lands. Where the weather could shift in the blink of an eye, the hills and trees were multiple shades of green. So many longed to call this place home. There was a magic about this land; Laga could feel it.

Laga had a perfect view of the land and the sea on top of the hill just north of the Point. She could see for miles and made a mental map of where she planned to explore next. The settlement's goats and sheep grazed nearby under the watchful eye of Donald, a young boy from the village who Laga had taken under her wing.

"Laga!" boomed Lars' voice, breaking Laga from her daydream.

"Brother, what do I owe the pleasure?"

"Why are you out here?" Lars demanded.

"I am taking the flock grazing. It's part of my job. I thought you knew that since you got it for me," Laga replied.

"You know damn well what I mean. You have ventured too far from the settlement."

"Please, Lars. I am not a child. I am perfectly capable of tending to the flock and myself. I have Donald; it is not as if I am alone."

Lars searched the hillside for the boy. The boy was barely of the breast, no more than twelve or thirteen winters. He was scrawny and looked like he would be scared of his own shadow. His hair was a red curling mop, and his skin was as fair as the snow back home. The boy was tending to an injured goat, bandaging its leg.

"Him? Laga, the goats could protect you better. Look, one of the goats is injured. This was a bad idea. I order you to return to the settlement at once," Lars boomed.

"You order me?" Laga smirked, raising one of her perfectly shaped eyebrows.

"Just because you see no sign does not mean the British troops are not nearby. Lief warns of war. The King has stopped by for a visit. Why else if the threat of attack is not imminent? You will not venture so far from the settlement from now on," Lars argued.

"Lars, I am not a child!" Laga snapped.

"While you are under my care, you will do as I say," Lars boomed before turning and heading back to the castle.

Laga watched him go, her blood boiling. She longed for the day when her brother would see her for the capable warrior she was. She longed for him to look at her the way he looked at the sword maidens. Yet she feared that all he would ever see her as was his baby sister and a farm hand.

"Laga, come," Donald called, snapping Laga from her resolve.

"What is it?" she asked.

Donald was a skinny, tall boy, all limbs with no muscle. The other village children had picked on him for not being very tough. Still, he was intelligent and good with the animals, so Laga offered to teach him how to tend the farm. The bullying stopped as soon as the Vikings took an interest in him.

"This goat, I am sure he is one of the twins. I still can't find his sister. I will keep looking but thought it best to inform you," he said.

"You did good, Donald, thank you. I will take it from here," Laga smiled, kneeling and stroking the goat's head.

The goat could stand; his injured leg didn't bother him much. That was a good sign. He would be no trouble returning home. Knowing the goat proved no issue, Laga's mind began to wander. This was her chance to explore. Lars couldn't be angry at her if animals vanished. It would make sense for her to follow up on a runaway.

The land was too enchanting and mysterious to not explore. What creatures did the woods hold? What other people called the land home? Laga had so many questions.

"Donald, you will not look alone. I shall accompany you," Laga smiled, scooping the goat into her arms and following the young boy.

"But Laga, what about Lars?" Donald worried.

"My brother's warnings are stupid. We are not going far, and we can still see the settlement from here. The kid must be nearby. She couldn't have gotten far."

Hesitantly, Donald nodded and led her up the hill. Adventure pulled at Laga like a siren's call. Her blood danced with excitement about what she might discover around every turn. She knew she should have been concerned when the clouds turned dark and the wind increased. But a storm just added to her curiosity. Uncertainty was part of the adventure, after all.

CHAPTER 2

THE STORM CAME in from the south, across the sea. The wind blew fast and hard, but even as the wind rose and thunder roared across the sky, Laga's concern was the missing goat. Continuing her hunt, Laga noticed tracks in the dirt. They led to the cliffs, where a collection of caves lay hidden in the trees.

"Laga, the storm is approaching fast; we should leave," Donald panicked.

"You head back with the rest of the flock. I will manage on my own."

"But Laga."

"But nothing, Donald. Your concern is touching, but I assure you I shall follow you home shortly," Laga smiled.

She had fast grown attached to the boy. Something about him rang true like he was a kindred spirit. She watched as he gathered the flock and led them back down the hill. Once she was sure he was close enough to home, she continued to follow the tracks before the oncoming rain washed them away.

The tracks led her deep into the woods, under thick, low, hanging branches and close to the overhang of the cliffs. She heard rustling and branches snapping underfoot and knew she was on the right path. It wasn't long before she found the baby goat in a crevasse. She had ventured quite a way from the rest of the flock, and Laga was sure if she hadn't searched for her, the poor goat would never have found its way back home. She would have likely become victim to the hounds who howled into the night.

"Come here, you little mischief maker," Laga chuckled, scooping the goat into her arms and checking her over.

Despite the rough and overgrown terrain, the goat was not hurt. Just then, a loud boom of thunder and a sharp flash of lightning startled both Laga and her small goat.

"I guess we better take shelter until the rain calms down," Laga said, stroking the goat's head to calm its racing heart.

The rain fell in heavy droplets, quickly soaking through Laga's clothes and making her shiver. She followed the path and ducked inside a low cave, crouching and squeezing inside like a child. She sat listening to the storm and watching how land reached for it, the way the trees bent in the wind, and the dry earth quenched its thirst by soaking up every hard drop of rain.

Since her legs were cramping and the wind was sending rain into the cave, Laga decided to venture deeper. She crawled along the cave floor before coming to an opening where she could comfortably stand, and she noticed the strange markings on the wall.

"I've never seen runes like these before. I wonder what they mean," Laga said. She had a habit of talking to her livestock.

Laga ran her fingers over the runes, trying to make a memory of them for later. They curved in ways she didn't understand. They had harsh lines and looked almost angry. Twisting in her gut told her these runes were important and needed to be investigated by someone who could read runes better than she could.

Sniffing the air, she sensed the faint smell of burning. Curiosity and longing for adventure clouded her usually sound judgement as she ventured deeper, following the scent.

Disappointment flooded her when all she found was the remains of a recent campfire.

"Nothing interesting or exciting about that," Laga grunted.

Heading back the way she came, she reviewed the carvings on the wall a little closer. They were not too deep and seemed like they were carved recently. Dust still gathered on the ledge below from where the rocks had been etched. She didn't know why but knew she had to tell Lars, even if he would disapprove of her disobeying his orders.

"Lars will have to wait until after the storm."

Taking a seat near the mouth of the cave, Laga cuddled the small goat until she felt it drift to sleep in her arms. She soaked in everything about the new area she had discovered. The sights, smells, and textures as she waited for the storm to end.

As soon as she deemed it safe, Laga headed back to town. Darkness approached, and she picked up her pace, feeling like she needed to report her findings urgently. Of course, she wanted to tell Lars. But truth be told, she wanted to talk to anyone, even Olga, about what she found. A part of her hoped it would be the start of everyone taking her seriously.

Laga let the little goat stretch its legs on the journey home. As she passed through town, her sights were on her little runaway, and she didn't see the cloaked stranger heading her way. Instead, she collided with his shoulder and felt a wall of muscle hidden by cloth.

"Apologies," Laga nodded, heading swiftly after the goat.

"Accepted," grunted a reply.

Laga looked over her shoulder at the cloaked stranger who had stopped to watch her. He lifted his head, briefly showing a small portion of his face. A short sharp blonde beard framed a strong jaw. There were beads braided into the longest part of his beard. A scar spread across one side of his cheek, leading to piercing blue eyes. His hair was cut close to his scalp while a long blonde braid cascaded over his shoulder.

The sight was enough for Laga to stop and take note. She knew her jaw had fallen open from the slight grin on his face, yet she couldn't move. She was frozen in place by the handsome stranger with a voice like gravel. She also didn't miss how he looked her up and down twice before swiftly turning and heading out of the village.

Who was he? She hadn't been at the settlement for long, but surely, she would remember seeing a face like that. Laga decided it was better to shrug it off. If he were from the village, she would see him again. Laga continued on her hunt for someone to inform about the runes.

CHAPTER 3

"Did I or did I not order you to come back home?" Lars roared.

"Lars, I am not a child. I might not be a Viking or a sword maiden, but I will knock you on your backside if you talk to me like that again," Laga snapped back.

If Laga didn't know better, she could be sure she saw an amused grin on her brother's face and, dare she say, a flash of respect?

"What is it about these runes that has you so excited? You can't even read runes," Lars insisted.

"I may not be able to read them, but I have seen enough to know these are different."

Laga pulled a blade from her boot and carved out the runes she could remember in the ground at their feet.

"They looked like this, and they were fresh; dust still lay on the ground," Laga insisted.

Lars examined the runes before rubbing a hand over his frustrated face. He folded his arms before straightening and sighing deeply.

"Laga, these are nothing to note. They are most likely from the Jarl Halfden. We all know of the havoc he wreaked before the King ended him. He probably carved them through Lief and his trail crew when he hid the Danegeld. Leave these things to the people who understand them. You just worry about your flock."

Lars pulled his sister to him and placed a gentle kiss on her forehead before leaving her to her thoughts. While his gesture was meant to be comforting, it enraged Laga. She might not be as well versed in these matters as Lars and his friends, but she knew she was right about the runes.

"What about the campfire? How do you explain that? It was far too fresh to be the Halfden's," Laga stormed after him.

"You took shelter from a storm; you can't be dense enough not to think others would have done the same. Now, it's getting late. Get some rest. You need it."

Laga watched her brother leave as her blood boiled. Why would no one ever take her seriously? Why would no one listen? Just because she was a shepherd, didn't mean she was a simpleton. She was intelligent, strong, and tough. She was a quick learner and had picked up more from Lars' stories of expeditions and raids than he knew. She had observed the sword maidens training enough to understand how to handle a sword. Her tactics might not be as successful as theirs, but she could handle herself. If it were not for her, the settlement wouldn't have food or wool to keep them warm in the winter. It vexed her that so many people dismissed her hard work.

"I need my rest? I'll show you who need rest," Laga mumbled after her brother.

Dissatisfied with his answer, Laga decided that if he would not go looking into the runes, she would. Even in the dead of night, she remembered the path. So, she took guard of the mouth of the cave from the tops of a tree, her movements hidden by the rustling of the leaves from the still blowing winds.

Who was there? What were they hiding? Was it an enemy? Or simply lovers hiding from prying eyes? She needed to know. She had noticed animals going missing from the settlement and the neighbouring villages. At first, she wondered if it was wolves. Still, now as the pieces of the puzzle fell into place, her mind opened up to the possibility that the predator in question was perhaps of the human variety.

She watched the cave long into the night, examining every shift in the shadows as closely as possible. However, little did Laga know that she was the one being watched.

CHAPTER 4

GUNNAR WAS A NORSEMAN, born and raised in Norway and a sworn enemy of the Danes. He and his fellow Norseman had camped at the Point many times over the previous several months. He had heard the locals who disapproved of his kind had tried to warn the Viking settlers of their presence. Gunnar found it amusing when they had dismissed such claims and assumed the camps were from a man they called Halfden, who had been rumoured to have sided with the Brits.

Stupid Vikings, always thinking they are so smart, Gunnar had thought.

They didn't even know he had breached their walls to investigate. He had passed so easily for one of their own, and none had batted an eyelid. They made his job too easy.

The leader of Gunnar's settlement had tasked him to find out as much as he could about the Danes. Was their settlement there to stay? Why were they here? What issues did they have with the Brits? And most importantly, were they a threat to the Norse settlement?

Gunnar's new home on the English shores lay much further down the rocky coast, far enough away where it shouldn't have been a concern. But the Vikings and the Norse had a checkered past. Any threat was still a threat, no matter how small.

Gunnar had passed his days sneaking into the Danish settlement and gathering information. At night, he would camp out in the shallow caves deep in the woods, hidden by the thickest section of trees and overgrown bushes.

The girl who now sat perched high in the trees scouting his hiding place was proving to be a problem. This was not the first time he had seen her there. And he was sure she would have reported what she found.

Gunnar stayed hidden in the shadows, watching her. She was beautiful for a Dane. Sharp features that could only be described as mean looking. A strong jaw with high cheekbones.

Dark almond eyes and ebony black hair travelled down her back and touched the back of her thighs. She was a strong woman, that much Gunnar could tell; even hidden under her heavy clothes, he knew she had a beautiful body.

She had clouded his mind ever since she had barged into him. Her eyes widened, and her jaw fell open when they locked eyes. He wouldn't forget it. Even so, her beauty was of no importance. She was a problem that needed to be solved. If she reported back and others came, Gunnar would be discovered, and threats would be imminent.

Gunnar liked that cave. It was tucked away, unseen unless one was looking for it. It was buried deep in the cliff, shielded from the harsh weather by the trees, and it was cosey enough for a cave. Now he would have to find somewhere else to camp at night.

Gunnar snuck off, leaving the girl to spy on an empty cave, to explore the cliff's edge higher up the hill. The caves there would be more exposed to the elements, but at least he would have a better vantage point if anyone did come looking. And it would be far enough away from the beautiful girl's prying eyes.

Perhaps a cliff closer to the settlement would be better. That way, if I am discovered, it's a quicker escape, Gunnar thought.

The storm earlier that day had come fast and true and left just as quickly. But just because it was only a short visit didn't mean the storm had not left its mark. Gunnar's boots squelched in the drenched earth, making the cliff edge slippery and treacherous. He needed to be careful. He couldn't see what lay below the cliffs at this time of night; it was much too dark. And he didn't fancy falling onto what could be a nasty path of jagged rocks that would most likely result in his death.

But caution on its own can be dangerous sometimes. Trying to avoid the edge, Gunnar didn't see the crack in the ridge. Instead, his weight sent the rocks below his feet tumbling and dragging him down. Gunnar clawed and dug his hands into the earth, trying to pull himself back up, but it was too wet from the rain, and the ground slid through his fingers.

Accepting his fate, he fell. The last thought on his mind was the girl.

This is all her fault: Nosey, interfering, beautiful Danish woman. Should have left well enough alone, Gunnar thought.

Her eyes flashed in his mind. The curve of her lips. Those thick, beautiful lips.

CHAPTER 5

THE LIGHT of a new day brought Gunnar back to his senses. He must have fallen and hit his head hard if he had been out all night. The light stung his eyes as he blinked them open. He was sure he saw something, but it took a while for his vision to adjust. Then, finally, he realised someone was kneeling over him. Not just anyone, but the raven-haired beauty from the night before.

"Are you hurt?" she gasped.

Gunnar ached from head to toe. His clothes were soaked and covered in mud; he wanted nothing more than a bath. He pushed himself to a sitting position and rubbed the back of his neck. He praised the gods that he had only bruises and cuts.

"I am fine," Gunnar lied. He tried to stand, but his ankle sent blinding pain coursing through him.

"You can't stand. You are hurt."

Gunnar said nothing, watching the girl closely. He could tell by her queering gaze and how her eyes roamed his body, examining his features and clothes, that she was trying to figure out what to do with him. Gunnar needed to think fast. He couldn't allow her to reveal his secret.

"Us Danes do not know the meaning of the word pain," Gunnar winched, forcing himself to stand.

The woman eyed him from head to toe. Gunnar kept his eyes on her face but didn't miss how her hand went to her hip. He knew she was reaching for a weapon.

"A misstep is all," Gunnar said.

He stepped to leave but could not stand and collapsed back to the floor.

"Looks like I won't be going anywhere for a while," Gunnar joked, hoping to crack the stone look she was giving him.

"Good, that means you can answer my questions," she grinned.

She sat opposite him, crossed her legs, and continued staring at him. He had to admire her determination.

"What is your name?" she asked.

"Gunnar."

"Where do you come from?"

"The settlement at the Point," Gunnar lied.

"Liar! I live there, and have never seen you," she snapped.

"You can't claim to know everyone. New people arrive all the time."

His response seemed to be enough for her. Her lips fell into a harsh straight line. She didn't know what else to say. She may not believe him, but she found it hard to deconstruct his lies. It was a simple lie. The best lies always are.

"I may not have met you, but my little spies know everyone. So, we shall see if your story rings true," Laga grinned, a wicked, knowing grin.

"You have no spies," Gunnar scoffed, trying to egg her into a fight to stop her from leaving. He needed more time to convince her.

"I do so. My little Donald goes through life ignored. People often dismiss him because he looks weak, but I was not fooled. He has proven himself invaluable," she stood and prepared to leave.

Donald? That name sounded familiar. Quickly Gunnar searched his mind. He had seen a young boy with flaming red hair who mostly tended to the animals. But he also had a way of getting himself into places children best not be seen. If anyone knew his story was a lie, it would be him. Gunnar couldn't let her leave.

"Wait!" Gunnar grunted, forcing himself to stand, grinding his teeth through the pain.

Gunnar took a step forward and grabbed her wrist. She snapped her head around to look at him, and once again, she looked at him like he was the only man in the world. Gunnar felt his pulse quicken and his body respond to her gaze. Fire started in his blood, a fire he hadn't felt before. It was intoxicating and intriguing.

"You never told me your name," Gunnar breathed, his eyes unable to leave her plush pink lips.

"Laga," she replied.

His breathing began to quicken at the flash of her tongue when she pronounced her name. Something was amiss, but in the best possible way. He had forgotten everything he was supposed to be doing or saying. Laga had him entranced. Gunnar couldn't help but notice how she hadn't pulled away, and her eyes now held a sparkle of lust.

"Laga," he whispered, feeling the word tingle on his lips.

A sudden urge came over him. A desire he couldn't and didn't want to ignore. Without knowing why, his grip on her wrist tightened, and he pulled her to him. Laga let out a small, almost inaudible gasp but didn't attempt to pull away or stop him. Gunnar didn't know if what he was about to do was a good idea or why he had chosen to do it. Laga had bewitched him, and he wanted more.

Entwining his fingers through her thick hair, he pulled her to him and brought his lips down to meet hers. Her lips were softer than anything he had felt before; she tasted of summer berries. The longer he kissed her, the more his body was set on fire. He felt like he was about to forget his duty and rip her clothes off when she responded by opening her mouth and allowing him to explore her mouth with his tongue. Laga's hands reached up, roaming over Gunnar's large biceps, down his torso, making him flinch as her fingertips grazed his hips, sending a tickle running through him.

Finally, they parted, gasping for breath but unable to remove their eyes from each other. Keeping her close, Gunnar stroked the back of her neck with his fingers.

"Please, Laga. Do not tell anyone I am here," Gunnar pleaded.

"Why not? What are you hiding?"

"I hide nothing. I simply had a disagreement with a fellow over a sword. Apparently, I had selected his sword from the blacksmith."

"Am I supposed to believe that?" Laga asked, her voice breathy.

"It was a simple misunderstanding. I can take care of myself, but this guy was much bigger than me and had a temper to boot. The blacksmith warned me not to get on the wrong side of him, and pride got the better of me. I have been camping out here to give him time to cool down before I talk with him again."

Laga's face grew serious once more. She didn't believe him; he needed to sell it harder. Laga also had questions of her own.

"So, you are a coward?" she teased.

"I am no such thing!" Gunnar snapped.

"The man I had the misunderstanding with doesn't like to play fair. I simply want him to cool down so we can talk man to man, alone away from his friends he likes to show off to."

Laga eyed him with suspicion, but Gunnar could feel her coming round to believing him.

"I can't exactly face a potential fight with my ankle in this state, can I?" Gunnar asked, allowing himself to stumble into her arms.

CHAPTER 6

LAGA STILL HAD HER SUSPICIONS. His story held some truth, but she couldn't get the runes out of her mind. Growing up with Lars had given Laga an understanding of Vikings and their foolish pride, so she was sympathetic to Gunnar's plight.

She knew she shouldn't trust him, but she couldn't help it; she liked that kiss. It had surprised her, enthralled her, when no one else had ever paid her much note. The voice in her mind told her to tread lightly; the kiss could be a ploy to distract her. But her body cried out to be listened to. Her body had responded to him so naturally. She also couldn't ignore the way she felt his body react to her. Someone had once told her, she couldn't remember who, that a man's growing manhood speaks the truth. Laga had felt his manhood pressed against her, making her mind cloudy with lust.

"I shall keep your presence secret for now."

"Thank you, Laga," Gunnar said, cupping her cheek and smiling back at her. "Your kindness will not go unnoticed."

His hand was rough against her skin, but she liked his touch. His hands were hard, but his touch was gentle. She wondered if he might venture for another kiss as she slowly moved closer, watching how he would react.

"Laga, I have been looking all over for you," Donald called, joining them in the clearing.

Startled, Gunnar and Laga swiftly moved apart, stunned by Donald's sudden intrusion. Donald stood staring as if waiting for an explanation.

"Who is your friend?" Donald asked.

Laga let out a breath she hadn't realised she was holding and smiled softly at Donald. She was thankful that Donald appeared not to know Gunnar. It was fortunate that the Scots didn't mix with the Vikings of the settlement much.

"I am sorry, have I not introduced you before?" Laga lied. "This is Gunnar, my cousin from Denmark. He arrived with the King."

"Finally found a way to get Lars to allow you to explore them?" Donald laughed.

Laga laughed her response and nodded, helping Gunnar to his feet.

Gunnar looked back at her, confused. She knew she could explain later. She hated lying to Donald, but loose lips had been known to sink ships, and she didn't want Donald speaking of a mysterious stranger he found Laga with when he got home.

"I have the flock with me...."

"Then we shall follow you on. We do not want the twins to sneak off again, do we?" Laga grinned.

Donald nodded and turned back in the direction of the flock. With the boy's gaze averted, Gunnar leant in closer. Laga could feel his breath tickle her neck and ear. She closed her eyes at the sensation that sent a thrill up her spine.

"Cousins?" Gunnar whispered down Laga's ear.

She had to admit it was a stupid lie. The way he looked at her was anything but cousinly. He took her hand and gently stroked his thumb over her knuckles. The sensation was seductive and set her skin ablaze. She wondered what it would feel like if he was to touch her like that somewhere else on her body.

CHAPTER 7

"WOULD A COUSIN TOUCH YOU LIKE THIS?" Gunnar breathed, grazing his lips down her neck as he wrapped his arms around her waist.

Laga allowed her head to fall back and rest on his shoulder. She was thankful for the flock keeping Donald busy and leaving them alone.

"Would a cousin touch you like this?" Gunnar asked again as his hands roamed her body, cupping her breasts.

Laga let out a small moan; she longed for his touch for reasons unknown to her. However, she decided not to question it. The best things in life had no explanation; that's what she had always believed.

Gunnar couldn't help but flirt with Laga. She was smart, sexy, and fun to be around. He liked how even though she fell for his lies, it took a lot to convince her, and she wasn't easily thrown by his good looks, even if she was falling for them now.

"Gunnar, stop. Donald might come back at any moment," Laga insisted.

"He is busy with your flock. You heard him say it yourself. Let us enjoy our time alone," Gunnar groaned, taking her earlobe between his teeth.

"What if someone from the village comes?" Laga asked.

Her question roused the spy in him. This could be the opportunity he had been looking for to gain the information he had yet to find. But, unbeknownst to Laga, she had let her guard down, and once a woman let her guard down around Gunnar, they were putty in his hands.

"Screw the village; let the Scots come. We can show them how the Danes make love."

"What if someone from the settlement finds us? They may find you," Laga breathed.

She was trying to fight her impulses. But, while her mouth argued her point, her body betrayed her, sinking into Gunnar's touch and moaning with pleasure as his fingers grazed her skin.

"No one of importance other than you would travel this way without meaning," Gunnar whispered.

"My brother might."

"Who is your brother?" Gunnar asked, spinning her to face him and burying his face in her neck.

"The second."

"The second is a man named Sven," Gunnar moaned.

"No, Sven left when they found the Dangeld stolen by Jarl Halfden. My brother Lars was sent by the King to be Lief's second in command. So that's how I came to be here."

Gunnar soon realised that the more Laga relaxed, the more her tongue did too. She was giving him everything he needed. She informed him of the plans to grow the settlement. Agreements of peace with the local Scots and how the King himself was still around, planning on leaving for Denmark in two days. So be it that he should indulge in a bit of romance. He was a hot-blooded male, after all. Who could blame him? And Laga wasn't complaining. She was savouring his every touch.

The more he tasted her skin, caressed her body, and explored her curves, the quicker he forgot about his mission. He had a new one; to make her scream his name. Gunnar backed Laga up against the wall of the cliff's overhang. Tearing at her clothes, he pulled out one of her ample breasts, taking it in his mouth as his other hand pulled up her skirts.

Laga bit her lip to stop herself from crying out in pleasure. Neither wanted to bring any attention to themselves lest their rendezvous be cut short. Gunnar felt himself growing and straining in his pants when his fingers found her entrance. She was wet, ready and willing to take him.

Gunnar slid one of his thick fingers inside her, thriving at the sound of her moans. He felt her clench around him; she was tight, perhaps a virgin. He longed to feel the rest of her and how tightly she could fit around him.

Lost in his quest for pleasure, a sudden twisting in his gut stabbed at him. Bile rose in the back of his throat. Guilt plagued his mind. Laga didn't deserve to be used in such a way. She could have easily turned him in, exposed him, and likely had him killed. Yet she had chosen not only to keep his presence secret but to lie to a trusted friend to protect him. Spying on her was one thing; indulging for the sake of information was another.

Why do I care? Gunnar asked himself.

Dare he say he was starting to care for the woman? Perhaps even love? No, surely not. It was too soon. Yet everyone knew how quickly the Vikings fell in love. That was no match for how fast and hard the Norsemen fell.

CHAPTER 8

"I SUSPECTED something was wrong when your bed had not been slept in, but when Donald said you were with a cousin who arrived with the King, I *knew* something was wrong!" Lars roared as he stormed through the tree line.

Their encounter came to an abrupt end. Laga pushed Gunnar away forcefully, making him stumble and wince at the pain from his ankle. Then, quickly fixing her clothing, she glared at her brother.

"What are you doing here, Lars?"

"Looking for you! What have I told you about venturing far from the settlement?"

"And I have told you I am not a child!" Laga roared back.

Lars opened his mouth to argue when his eyes drifted over to Gunnar. Only a second before, the man had been dishevelling his sister. To Lars, this man was a threat to his family.

"So, who is this man you claim to be our cousin?" Lars snarled, eyeing Gunnar up and down.

"I am Gunnar from the settlement. I arrived months past," Gunnar lied.

"What is your rank?" demanded Lars.

"I am a warrior," Gunnar answered, standing proud.

Lars drew closer, his gaze burning into Gunnar. Laga may

have been fooled by this man, but Lars would be harder, if not impossible, to convince.

"I was introduced to every warrior who called this land home on my arrival, and I have met everyone who has landed since," Lars snarled.

"Lars, what are you saying?" Laga asked.

"I am saying this man is a stranger, a liar, and not who he claims to be," Lars spat back.

Laga stood bewildered, watching the exchange between the two men. Gunnar's eyes raged, his knuckles white on clenched fists, but he was yet to make a move. Lars looked like he was about to rain down a world of terror on Gunnar if he didn't speak soon. Laga's heart raced; she knew something was wrong but had let her lust and longing cloud her judgement. She felt like a fool.

"I am Gunnar. I live in the settlement. I have been hiding after a dispute with a brother," Gunnar lied again.

That's when Lars's face flushed as if he remembered something.

"I know you; you are the stranger lurking around camp. I saw you at the castle. You said you were meeting the blacksmith, yet the blacksmith has his own dwelling outside the castle grounds. Everyone in the settlement knows that, especially the warriors who use him for their blades!" Lars' voice rose with every word, his anger burning like the sun.

Lars shoved Gunnar hard. Gunnar limbed back a step, struggling to stand on his still aching ankle.

"Tell me who you are!" Lars roared.

"Lars, stop!" Laga pleaded.

"Laga, it is fine," Gunnar interrupted.

That's when it happened. Gunnar's secret was exposed. When Gunnar turned his head to comfort Laga, his collar slipped, exposing the harsh curved lines of a rune. A rune that Lars had seen before, a rune that resembled what Laga had seen in the cave. Lars launched forward, grabbing Gunnar by the throat.

"Norseman scum!" Lars roared.

Instinct kicked in, and Gunnar punched Lars hard in the face. Lars let go as his nose began to bleed.

"Your blood is not worthy to taste my blade. I shall beat you with my bare hands!" Lars bellowed.

Charging at Gunnar, Lars unleashed several fast attacks, punching Gunnar across the jaw and splitting the skin in several places. Gunnar's beard turned red as his blood soaked into his hair.

"Lars, stop! What are you saying?" Laga cried, pushing her brother away from Gunnar and jumping between the two men.

"Are you blind, sister? The rune on his neck, it is the same as the cave. It means he is Norseman," Lars roared back.

Laga turned sharply around to Gunnar. All lust, trust, and compassion left her face, replaced by betrayal and blind rage. It was a fury to rival her brother's. Gunnar looked back at her, startled as her piercing eyes bore down, burning deep into him. Guilt rose once again in his gut.

"Is it true?" Laga demanded.

"Laga, let me ex...."

"Is it *true*!" Laga yelled.

Gunnar let his head drop in defeat. He couldn't bear to look at the hurt and anger in her eyes. His shoulders slumped, and he nodded he answer.

The hillside was steep, exposed to the high winds from the shore below the cliffs. Even though the thicket of trees, the ground had been exposed to the elements. The ground was soaked, making it easy to sink into the mud under their weight. Lars had been right. Just because you couldn't see a threat, it didn't mean one wasn't there.

"You lied to me! I let you touch me!" Laga roared.

"Laga, I'm...."

"I do not want to hear another venomous word from your lips!" Laga thundered, shoving Gunnar with all her might.

The hillside was hard enough to travel when soaked from a storm. Gunnar couldn't stay steady on his injured ankle. The force of Laga's shove, compiled with him not being prepared, made him fall back and roll down the hill quickly. Tumbling head over heels, Gunnar descended towards the cliffs.

Laga's watched in horror, filled with hurt and wonder, as Gunnar fell uncontrollably closer to danger. Gunnar scrambled, trying to steady himself, grabbing at anything he could to stop his fall, but nothing helped. The ground came up in his hands, tree roots buckled under him, and before he knew it, he toppled over the cliff's edge.

Laga gasped when Gunnar disappeared from sight. With him gone, the reality hit her all at once. Tears burst from her eyes like a tidal wave at sea. Her heart constricted. She had never felt pain like it before. Was it heartbreak? Betrayal? Or something deeper?

CHAPTER 9

GUNNAR SPLASHED into the icy waters below. Even in summer, the waters of England were as cold as winter. Swimming back to shore, Gunnar replayed the events in his mind. He supposed he deserved Laga's outburst. He had lied to her, used her, and yes, it was true; he had betrayed her. But he couldn't blame her. He knew women who had killed for less.

Pulling himself back onto shore, he looked up at the cliff from which he fell. He half expected to see Lars and Laga checking to see if he had died in the fall. But no one stood atop the cliff.

Deciding there was no more he could do, he made his way back up the shore towards home. What could he do? She had made her feelings clear. She was a Dane, and he was a Norseman. Sworn enemies. It was not as if they could make a life together. Neither of their people would allow it. Besides, he had what he came for, even if he got the information underhandedly. His mission was complete. He now had to report back to his Chieftain.

The distance between the Norse settlement and the Vikings was at least a two-day ride. It was going to take even longer by foot. Thankfully, Gunnar knew of several caves he could rest in along the way. But unfortunately, his ankle cried out with every step, slowing him down. The uneven shoreline didn't help. But

Gunnar didn't have time to complain or rest. He had been exposed; it was only a matter of time before the Vikings raged war.

War with the Vikings was the least of Gunnar's worries. When his ankle became too much to bear, he made his way towards the hills, hunting for a place to rest, and ran straight into a battalion of British troops. They were armed for battle and out for blood.

Gunnar was unarmed and vastly outnumbered. He would be a fool to try and fight his way free. Staring down sat a soldier on a large white horse. Gunnar stood still, silent, waiting.

"Grab him. He is Viking!" ordered the soldier.

Gunnar was swiftly surrounded and forced to his knees, his hands bound, and a foul-tasting rag was tied around his mouth. A soldier pulled down his collar, exposing the rune on his neck.

"This one is Norseman," yelled another soldier.

"It matters not. They are all the same. Take him!" ordered the one in command.

As soldiers forcefully dragged Gunnar towards the British camp, his mind raced. This was Laga's fault. He wouldn't have walked right into the British troop's path if she had not forced him over the cliff. But then anger turned to concern. They were heading towards the Point, directly to the settlement. Was this the only battalion? What was their plan? As Gunnar was shoved into a tent, his mind turned to Laga. He needed to escape. He needed to warn her. Protect her.

CHAPTER 10

STUPID BRITS, Gunnar amused himself.

The troops had left him alone, underestimating him purely because he was alone. Moreover, the soldier who had bound him didn't do a very good job, giving Gunnar the perfect opportunity to wriggle free and escape.

Slipping out, he made his way through the maze of tents heading back home. When he reached a tent that was ornately decorated, he stopped. He never could understand the use of such decoration. It was like a beacon for enemies to target. Guards stood outside, protecting against enemy attack. Gunnar wasn't concerned, all he needed to do was get a sword or axe, and he could take them both easily and be gone before anyone noticed.

Gunnar crouched behind a supply barrel, waiting for the coast to be clear for him to make a run for it when a conversation tickled his ear.

"When we are done, the Point will be a beacon of warning for all the other scum trying to claim our land as their own. They will be able to see the flames from the Norse settlement. By the time any of them have figured out what's going on, there will not be enough of them left to stand against us."

Multiple voices chuckled their approval.

"What are our targets?" asked a voice.

"There are two Viking settlements in the area, one at the Point and one just beyond by the eastern coast. If you travel down the coast towards the south, and there is a Norse settlement...."

Gunnar stopped listening. They were talking about his home and Laga's. He needed to know more, but he couldn't risk waiting outside and being seen with men walking around heavily armed. A cough and feet dragging in the dirt caught Gunnar's attention. One of the guards from the front of the General's tent had separated. From how the man jerked his leg and pulled at his groin, it was clear to Gunnar he was heading to relieve himself. Gunnar stuck to the shadows, following the man into the cover of the trees at the edge of the cap. Gunnar waited until the man had his pants around his ankles, in a vulnerable position with his dick in his hand, before he made his strike.

Sneaking up from behind, Gunnar grabbed the man's sword, wrapping his arm around his throat. Gunnar rested the troop's manhood on the top of the blade.

"One word, and I make you a woman," Gunnar snarled. Then, looking down, Gunnar laughed low in his throat. "From your size, no wonder you Brits are so angry."

"Foreign scum, I will have your head," the guard growled.

"Castrated with your own sword, I hope you already have children," Gunnar replied, digging the blade deeper into the man's groin.

"Tell me what you know. What are the General's plans for the settlements?" Gunnar demanded, keeping one ear on the camp behind.

"I'm not telling you a thing!" spat the guard.

Gunnar spun him around, tossing the troop into a tree. The man groaned and gasped as the force of the hit forced the air from his lungs. Gunnar pounced, pinning the man to the tree. Gunnar pressed his arm deeper into the man's neck, the sword still trained on its target.

"I do not like repeating myself. Answer my questions, or I

have no more use for you, and killing you will be my entertainment," Gunnar snarled.

The troop gulped loudly, nodding his understanding. Gunnar released the man's neck a touch, giving him room to speak.

"The General acts on orders above my station. I can only tell you what I know. We plan on ridding our lands of all foreign invaders. The Vikings, the Norse, all of them."

"You are holding back, and I am losing my patience," Gunnar snarled, digging the blade closer and drawing a small line of blood.

The troop winced before chuckling and glaring Gunnar dead in the eye.

"Kill me if you must. I swore my life to the course. If I die, as a result, it will be a death of honour, be it defending our plans or by the sword in battle."

"Bleeding out from where your tiny cock once stood by your own sword is honourable to you? You Brits are a strange people," Gunnar provoked.

"It makes no difference; all is fair in war," the troop spat.

"War?" Gunnar asked.

"War is imminent. You cannot stop it. The settlement at the Point will be the first hit. After that, the fires will rage and be a warning to others like you of what is to come! Norseman filth," The guard sneered.

"When?" Gunnar snapped.

"Sooner than you think," laughed the guard.

Gunnar spun the blade clobbering the troop over the head with the hilt. Making sure the man was out cold, Gunnar headed straight home with as much urgency as he could. He was almost entirely out of sight of the British camp when he was plagued with an attack of consciousness.

I can't leave Laga and the Vikings knowing what I know. It is not the honourable thing to do. But they are Vikings, our sworn enemy. I can't betray my people for one pretty face. Gunnar argued with himself.

Gunnar went back and forth, pacing through the trees fighting with himself before he made a choice. No man of honour would betray an enemy when a bigger enemy was coming to light. Even if the Norsemen hated the Vikings and vice versa, they needed all the numbers they could get to prepare for war.

Gunnar hobbled back to the camp as quickly as he could, ignoring the pain of each step. The horses were tied on the edge of the camp, left grazing and unguarded. Gunnar grabbed the first horse he could and made his way to Laga.

CHAPTER 11

LAGA AND DONALD SAT QUIETLY, watching the flock on the outskirts of the settlement. The grass was greener outside the settlement walls. It was a peaceful night. The storm the previous day had cleared the air. There was not a cloud in sight. The stars sparkled in a black velvet sky while the moon illuminated the top of the hill. That's when Laga saw it. A man on horseback charged down the hill with urgency. As the figure drew closer, her heart began to pound in her chest. It was Gunnar.

"What is the name of the gods, both new and old, are you doing here?" Laga demanded, though her voice was less threatening than she planned.

"Leave the flock and get back to the settlement now. Where is your brother? The others in command? I must speak with them immediately!" Gunnar rambled as he dismounted.

"You are a known Norseman now. They will kill you on sight before you even utter a word. Besides, why should I help you after how you treated me?" Laga snapped, all memories of his betrayal flooding back.

"Laga, we do not have time. One my way home to my settlement...."

"Your settlement? There is a Norseman settlement? Where? Is it close?" Laga asked frantically.

"Laga! There is no time. I was captured by the British. An army is coming. They plan on attacking and burning the settlement to the ground. They attack here first, then the other Viking settlement before they come for my people. We need to warn everyone."

Gunnar panicked.

"An army? That can only mean...."

"Yes, war. Our people may be enemies, but now we have a common enemy. We need to band together and fight. Separated, our people do not stand a chance. Together we may still taste victory."

A boot snapped a twig on the floor, startled Gunnar and Laga turned to see Lars emerging from the darkness. His face was no longer angry or disgusted but full of concern.

"Why? Why come back and offer to help us?" Lars asked, standing firmly at Laga's side.

Gunnar looked to Laga and knew only the truth would set him free.

"Believe me when I say I didn't come by the decision lightly. I was travelling home to warn my people when....my mind raced to Laga. I love her. The thought of those British rats harming her or someone she loves sickened me. But, I am a man of honour. So, I can put my grievances with the Vikings aside for a greater cause....and the love of a good woman," Gunnar answered, bowing his head to Lars.

Lars stood silently, eyeing Gunnar with suspicion.

"You think me a fool? You have used my sister once. You dare use her again?" Lars snarled, anger beginning to burn in his eyes.

Laga stepped in front of her brother, placing a gentle hand on his chest, calming him.

"I believe him, Lars. He could have run and to his own people first. But instead, he comes to an enemy camp, outnumbered by many who could kill him simply for being. Instead, he offers a truce out of love for me. Father would have done the same for Mother."

Lars's eyes snapped to his sister. He was frozen, unknowing what to say.

"Go back to the settlement, warn the others. Prepare for war. Donald and I shall bring in the flock with the dogs."

"I shall go with you. To prove I am no liar," Gunnar said.

Reluctantly, Lars nodded.

CHAPTER 12

LIEF, Lars, and the others stood in the great hall waiting for news. Gunnar paced anxiously back and forth while Laga sat watching him closely, her heart aching at the concern on his face. The room was so silent that no one dared talk. A lot had already been discussed, and if the scouts didn't confirm Gunnar's story, he would be put to death. Finally, dawn peeked over the horizon, turning the great hall shades of orange and yellow. Talks had gone on all evening, to the point everyone was sick of their own voices. Now it was just a waiting game.

Seconds felt like minutes; minutes felt like hours before suddenly the doors burst open. Four riders ran in panting, panicked looks painting their faces.

"Out with it!" Lief roared.

"The Norseman speaks the truth. There is a British camp not far from here. No more than a day's ride at least," answered one of the riders.

"How many?" Lars asked.

"Thousands, and we fear more may be coming."

The room erupted into a roar of voices, stomping feet, and weapons drawn.

"Silence!" Lief roared. "War approaches. Prepare the settlement's defences. Evacuate the woman and children. Warn the neighbouring village, now!"

"I need to go home and warn my brothers. I will do my best to convince my people to join the fight. The British are our enemy too."

"I shall join you. It will take one of our leaders to show we are in earnest," Lars nodded, offering Gunnar his hand.

"Brother," Gunnar nodded.

Laga's heart felt like it was being ripped from her chest. She wasn't a fighter, not in the traditional sense. She would be evacuated with the other woman, and Gunnar was leaving. Unable to watch him vanish from sight again in less than two days, she turned to leave. Goodbye had always been a word she couldn't say.

"Where are you going?" Gunnar asked, grabbing Laga's arm.

"You heard Lief. I have my orders."

"Come with me," Gunnar asked.

Laga spun around to face him. Her eyes were filled with tears of hope as she looked back into Gunnar's ice blue eyes.

"I cannot enter this war not knowing where you are. Not knowing you are safe. I want you to come home with me....as my wife."

EPILOGUE

THE ENTIRE WORLD WAS CHANGING. Vikings and Norseman may soon be banding together, sworn enemies now allies. A war they had tried to prevent had found its way to their door. The British might have the numbers, but Lars was sure they didn't have the fighters, not like the Danes and the Norse.

It was a day and a half's ride from the Point to Gunnar's settlement. Another storm loomed over the coast. The group had hoped they could find shelter before the storm hit, but the path of love and war was never an easy one to take.

Rain poured down so hard it hurt the skin. The wind howled and hit like a punch to the jaw. The horses struggled through the soft earth before a cave came into view. They couldn't go on until the storm had passed. They all prayed it would sail by as quickly as the last. With the horses tied, bellies fed, and a small fire keeping the group warm, Lars pulled his furs close and settled in for some much-needed rest. Gunnar stood watch, on guard for any British troop who might venture by.

"Would you like some company?" Laga asked coyly.

"From my beautiful wife-to-be? Always." Gunnar grinned and opened his arms wide, pulling Laga close.

Young love was so sweet and new. Like youngsters tasting love's sweet nectar for the first time, the conversation turned from war to admiration rather quickly. Flirtatious words, hearty laughs, and smouldering looks were exchanged between the two as the heat ramped up in the cave.

Lars leapt to his feet, startling the two love birds.

"You two are disgusting."

"We are in love," Laga chimed.

"I would rather pace out in the rain than be forced to listen to you two much longer. Talks of sweet nothings, talks of woo. I've heard enough. I will watch from outside. I shall see you both at dawn."

Lars grumbled to himself as he left the cave. His shadow travelled back and forth as he patrolled outside. Finally alone, Laga realised the heat was not simply from the fire that crackled at her back; it was the heat between herself and Gunnar.

Every chance they had to be alone had been interrupted, cut short before she could feel him the way she craved. Now was Laga's chance.

"We are all alone, uninterrupted for once, it may seem," Laga teased.

"Whatever shall I do with you?" Gunnar growled, burying his face in Laga's neck, nipping at her soft skin as his hands roamed her body.

Laga stood, taking Gunnar's hand and leading him deeper into the cave, away from Lars.

"You know, I suppose this is our wedding night," Laga whispered as she nipped playfully at Gunnar's ear.

"Then let me show you how Norsemen consummate our marriages," Gunnar growled. His voice was dark and tantalising.

Gunnar entwined his fingers into Laga's hair, stroking the back of her neck, claiming her as he pulled her in. His lips melted into hers. Laga responded, opening her mouth to receive him, their tongues entangled in a passionate embrace.

Gunnar's hands travelled from her hair, learning every curve of her body. Gunnar cupped Laga's round buttocks squeezing tightly until she moaned in his mouth. Picking her up, Gunner groaned with pleasure. Laga wrapped her legs around his waist and her arms around his neck. Gunnar carried her over to a bolder, placing her on top. Slowly he lifted her skirts, stroking his rough hands over her soft skin, savouring every inch of her.

"Do you have other clothes in your travel bag?" Gunnar whispered in her ear.

Laga nodded. Before she could blink, Gunnar grinned against her lips, gripping her cotton shirt, tearing it down the middle, exposing her ample breasts to him. His cock bulged between his thighs at the sight of her. Then, pulling himself free, Gunnar wasted no time thrusting into her.

Laga moaned at the sensation of him stretching her, filling her completely. Gunnar wasn't too big, but he was broad. With each slow stroke, Laga's chest heaved. He fit her perfectly as if he was made for no one else but her. His strokes were slow at first; he was careful not to hurt her. But when her moaning grew louder, Gunnar found it increasingly hard to control himself. He needed to feel her come apart around him, to soak in her juices and feel her claim him as her own.

Taking her nipples in his mouth, Gunnar thrust faster and faster. Laga bit her lip to stop herself from screaming. The sound of their pleasure was etching from the cave walls. Laga tore at Gunnar's shirt, eager to free him, to feel his flesh on hers. She gasped as she ran her hands over his chest. Compared to the Vikings, she knew he was not the biggest, but his definition was unmatched. She had never seen muscles like it.

Her nails tore at his shoulders as her climax took hold. Her head fell back as she moaned out his name, squeezing him and milking his seed as his own pleasure ripped through.

Gunnar slumped at her shoulder, kissing her neck softly as he regained his breath.

"Now it is my turn to show you how we Danish women do it," Laga breathed in his ear.

Pushing him softly, Laga stepped down from the boulder, her legs still trembling. She nodded at his clothes, wordlessly telling him to strip. She wanted to enjoy all of him. Eyes locked, they freed themselves from their remaining clothes.

Laga lay on the cave floor, spreading her legs wide, giving Gunnar a full mesmerising view of her. Their pleasure was still present on her inner thighs. Beckoning for him to join her, Laga traced one of her breasts, teasing herself for him. Gunnar sank to his knees and crawled on top of her.

Gripping his shoulders, she pushed him around and crawled on top of him, straddling his hips. Sinking herself onto him, Laga cried out in ecstasy. Gunnar reached up, taking her breasts in his hands. He teased her nipples between his fingers as Laga slowly began to grind her hips. Arching her back, Laga reached behind, resting her hands on Gunnar's muscular thighs. Her rhythm changed, and with each movement, she pulled him deeper. Gunnar felt like he might go mad with pleasure. This woman was like no one he had ever met before. Gunnar reached down between her legs, his thumb searching for the sweet spot. He needed to drive Laga wild. He teased her aching bud; with each motion, Laga picked up speed until they were both ready to come apart. Her muscles tingled as her pleasure grew until her body was overtaken with pleasure, sending her vision white as Gunnar moaned her name.

Panting, sweating, and unable to tear their eyes from each other, they lay side by side. But Gunnar wasn't finished yet.

"One more," he whispered as his hand slid down her chest to her hips.

"More?" Laga gasped, both in shock and excitement.

"I want to hear my name bounce off these walls."

Gunnar began to trail kisses across her stomach, down her inner thigh, and back up her other leg. Then, pushing her legs open, his fingers teased her opening. He grinned, watching her squirm and writhe at his touch, her hands massaging her breasts. He loved watching her.

Laga felt his breath warm her, teasing the neat mound of hair decorating her. She ached and longed for his touch. His teasing was maddening. She moaned as his tongue lapped over her aching bud; this was better than anything she had ever experienced. His tongue danced over her, and his fingers thrust and stretched her. Laga gripped his blonde hair tightly, struggling to control her pleasure as the heat built in the pit of her stomach. Her breathing quickened as he brought her closer and closer to the release she craved.

"Gunnar," she moaned.

"Louder," he breathed into her, his deep voice sending vibrations over her, adding to her pleasure.

"Gunnar....Gunnar.....Gunnar!" Laga cried out as her ecstasy took hold.

His name echoed throughout the cave as her glory glistened on his lips.

THE END

Did you enjoy the Gunnar and Lana's story?

Please review it on Goodreads, or Bookbub.

LARS

CHALLENGED BY THE MAIDEN

PROLOGUE

THE RAIN HAD NEVER BOTHERED Lars. If anything, he found the rain cascading down his face therapeutic and cleansing. Raising his face to the heavens, Lars stood thinking, letting the cold winds and the rain wash away his worries. But the longer he stood, his mind raced, leaving him anxious. No amount of rain would wash away his fears that night.

Moving from Denmark to England had been an easy choice. The settlement was supposed to be an easy posting – helping Leif build and grow the new settlement at the Point. Lars had hoped it would be a step in the right direction to becoming one of the King's trusted few. So, how did he end up here?

Summoned by the King to inform him of the latest developments in the British Isles, Lars was tasked with working on a plan for the upcoming war with the British. The task seemed simple enough. Yet here he was on the journey to an entire settlement of Norsemen without backup. Lars prided himself on being "in the know." So the fact that he had been at the settlement for almost a year and not known the Norse were but a stone's throw away was a blow to the ego. What else didn't he know? As doubts crept in, Lars became more unsettled.

Pacing back and forth in front of the cave, his stomach twisted with worry. The Norse were a lifelong enemy, and he felt woefully unprepared. He would be riding into the mouth of the beast with no warriors by his side. In hindsight, Lars knew if he had arrived with force, his words would have fallen on deaf ears. It would have been viewed as an act of aggression resulting in unnecessary bloodshed.

He glanced back to the cave where Laga and her new husband were up to things Lars didn't want to contemplate. Lars hoped and prayed to the gods that his new brother-in-law held the power to get him an audience with the right person.

Laga's laugh echoed through the cave, washing over Lars with a momentary feeling of happiness. Laga was his world. Her protection and happiness had always been a priority. Lars might not have agreed with the union initially, but Gunnar's love for Laga was undeniable. He could have let them all die at the hands of the Brits. Instead, he came back to help out of his love for Laga. Lars longed to have someone who loved him so.

Regret reared its ugly head. Lars had been close to love once back home in Denmark with a beautiful maiden with golden hair. They were set to marry. But on hearing his orders from the King to venture to the British Isles, she ran into the arms of another.

Should I have fought harder for her before she wed? Did I make a mistake letting her go? Lars thought as he continued to pace.

Shaking off the thought, he told himself it hadn't been a mistake. This was his destiny, his chance for glory, and his life's ambition of working for the King. Besides, what did Lars know of love?

CHAPTER 1

Triska sat glaring at Gunnar and his guests. She was in no mood for pleasant introductions with the Viking enemy. How could her most trusted spy have arrived after his mission not only with a new wife but with a *Dane*? Triska had fought all her life to prove she was up to the task of being a woman in charge of a Norse settlement. Having one of her own bring a sworn enemy into camp for an audience would likely bring her rule into question. This meeting was the last thing she needed.

Gunnar confidently explained himself, fighting his case for siding with the Danes against the British. But all Triska could do was look back at the tall bulking Dane. Lars indeed had large, broad shoulders that tapered down to a trim waist. His arms were so strong his clothes looked like they would tear open given the proper movement. He had a long black beard that travelled past his chest, tidied in twists and braids. He was far too distracting for Triska's liking.

"I need no help repelling the British. They pay us no mind; let them bother the Danes. One less thing for us to worry about. Let our enemies kill themselves. The British are not my problem," Triska stated.

Her council of warriors erupted with cheer at her announcement. Her men were loyal and trusted her guidance; after all, she had protected them so far.

"They may not be your problem now, but they will be," the mountain of a man argued back.

"Really? And what makes you so sure?"

"The British do not see us as Norsemen or Viking. They see us as invaders on their land. They do not care about our history. To them, we are the same."

"Ha! We are nothing alike. You Vikings are brutes, all brawn and no brain. We Norse are far superior in every way. Ask your sister, she spent her life with Vikings, yet beds with the Norse," Triska teased, enjoying the struggle on the Viking's face.

Triska knew she had touched a nerve; all she needed was to push him that much harder. Once Lars lost his temper and attacked, she would have no concern about her men wanting to side with him.

"You prove my point. Why should the British view us differently if a Viking woman can pair with a Norse? You may leave us to battle the Brits alone, but how long do you think it will be before they knock on your door?" Lars warned.

Triska's men mumbled amongst themselves. The Dane had a point. Triska sat silently watching as he fought his case to her men. He wasn't backing down. Triska forced herself to suppress a small smile. Dane or not, she admired his determination and drive. He was willing to put himself at the mercy of his enemies to help his people. He was a strong Viking, both mentally and physically. But she was stronger and longed for the day she would prove that point to him.

"Let's say what you speak is true, and the British come for our home," Triska started. "Why should we help you? We have lived here unbothered by the British far longer than you Vikings. The Brits were no problem until you invaded. If anything, the problem is your fault. You made your bed; now is the time to lay in it!" Triska snapped over the growing roar of her men.

CHAPTER 2

"WE STOPPED the war from escalating. We killed the traitor who sided with the British...." Lars argued.

"Exactly! One of your own betrayed you. It was *your* kind who brought on this war in the first place. Why should I put the lives of my people in your hands!? You would sooner sink your axe in my back than die protecting the people who fight beside you!" Triska retorted. She jumped to her feet and stormed across the tent to stand nose to nose with Lars.

"Do not claim to know me! Accusations of such treachery do not fall gently with me!" Lars roared.

"What do you plan on doing to stop me, *Dane*?" Triska yelled back.

The tent fell silent. Everyone stood watching the exchange. Lars clenched his jaw, looking into Triska's deep brown eyes. He could see how she was enjoying tormenting him. She wanted him to beg for her help; Lars would rather die.

The Norse woman stood to the same height as Lars. Her deep brown hair was pinned back in multiple braids keeping it out of her face. Her arms held almost as much muscle as his own. Lars found he admired her definition and the fact she was dressed for battle, armed with two broad swords at her hips.

"Oh, look, the Dane has lost his tongue. Nothing else to say? Because you know I speak the truth!" Triska taunted.

"How can you claim we invaded these lands if you were here first?" Lars snarled back, matching her whit.

"The Brits paid us no mind until your kind came along," she answered.

"My King does not want a full-scale invasion – Not until our settlements have a secure foothold in the North. It is just payment for betraying us. You claim to have no ill blood with the British, but they told your spy that they plan on coming for you next. Why is that?" Lars asked, a self-satisfied grin creasing his lips.

"You Danes are fools. You claim you need our help, then tell us your King's plan for these lands."

"Deflecting. I tell you this as an offer of trust. The enemy of my enemy is my friend. Do you wish to be our friend in this war or our enemy?" Lars questioned.

"Say, for instance, we help you. When you make your invasion, where does that leave us?" Triska inquired.

"I cannot speak for my King. I promise that if you join us, I will do everything possible to ensure we can live in peace."

"And I am supposed to accept your word?"

Lars felt his temper flaring. All this arguing was wasting time. While they stood debating, the British took a step closer to burning down his home. Lars couldn't understand why this beautiful and strong woman could be so careless with her people's lives. The Danes had two settlements; the Norse had one. Numbers alone should make her want to join him.

Stupid stubborn Norse, making a constant mess of things, Lars thought.

"You are supposed to want to protect your people. War is coming, yet you are willing to stand back?" Lars yelled.

"How dare you come to me for help then stand in my home and insult me. All I do is think of my people, which is why I want nothing to do with your war!" she snapped back.

Tempers flared, and words flew like daggers as their argument continued. Was it hatred for each other or something else that had them fighting with such unbridled passion for their cause?

"Enough!" the woman roared, "I have said what I needed; now take your leave."

"You are a fool," Lars shot back.

"Then call me a fool…"

"British attack!" yelled a voice from outside as the war horn was blown. The last thing Lars saw before Triska left the tent was a look of blazing fury directed at him as she pulled both swords and joined the fight.

CHAPTER 3

TRISKA RAN out of her tent to see British troops running through her settlement like an army of annoying ants. The attack couldn't be timed more perfectly. It was as if the British knew the Vikings and Norse were arguing amongst themselves. She had allowed Lars to distract her and planned on making him pay for that later.

Triska ran through the settlement, barking orders to her soldiers. "Formation, shields, arms!" They may not have been prepared for this attack, but that would not stop them from defending their home.

Triska's attacks were unrelenting; as soon as a solider would block her broadsword, leaving himself open, she would thrust her short sword into his gut, slicing him open and leaving him dead. Brandishing two swords made it easier to fight against such numbers. The British troops were no match for her. Her eyes darted from opponent to opponent. She was braced for every attack before it came.

Blocking an attack on two fronts, Triska pulled her arms wide, bringing her swords around with such speed that the troops she fought were unprepared. Her blades sliced through their throats, and blood sprayed over her as the men fell to the floor, gripping their necks hopelessly, trying to cling to life.

Footsteps behind her alerted Triska to another presence. Spinning around with her sword drawn, she stopped her blade just in time as it met with Lars' throat.

"What are you still doing here, Dane?" Triska snapped.

"A simple thank you would be nice," Lars retorted.

Pulling a knife from his hip, Lars tossed it through the air flying past Triska's ear, embedding itself in the throat of an attack from behind.

"I do not want nor need your help," Triska barked as she fought a short-round soldier who was not fit for battle.

"I warned you the British would come," Lars refuted.

"You came here for your selfish reasons. Do not claim anything else."

"You are hopeless," Lars exclaimed.

"The British never bothered us until you rode into camp!"

Triska fought men on both fronts. Lars wielded his axe with impressive skill. But Triska couldn't allow herself to become distracted by him. She was still enraged by his earlier words. Now, her home was under attack. If he insisted on staying, he would be forced to listen to her. As they fought side by side, Triska argued her point, only for Lars to refuse to back down on his. They were caught in a never-ending battle, one of swords and one of words.

Engrossed in battle, the two warriors turned, and Triska's swords came crashing down to meet Lars' axe. Entwined in a battle embrace, they locked eyes as they panted for breath.

"Hold your tongue, woman. How is a man supposed to fight with all this talking?" Lars growled, shoving her back to focus on the fight.

"Typical Viking male. No head for more than one task at a time," Triska laughed as she took the head clean off a soldier barely out of manhood.

A pause in battle came on them. No troops ran their way, the numbers dwindling against the forces of the Norsemen. Triska looked out over her settlement. The place lay in ruin, but her people handled the remaining troops well. A hand grabbed her arm, calling her attention. She turned to see Lars with a face like thunder but with lust and longing filling his eyes.

"No head for more than one task?" Lars asked, flinging another knife through the air and striking down a soldier in the distance as he pulled Triska to him. His lips hammered down on hers as his tongue invaded her mouth. For a second, she lost her thoughts and kissed him back until she felt him smiling against her lips. Shoving him away, Triska sheathed one of her swords, slapping Lars hard enough on the cheek to leave him as red-faced as she felt.

"You do not know your place," she snapped but found she couldn't bring herself to pull her gaze from his mouth.

Without thinking, Triska grabbed Lars by the collar and pulled him back to her. A thrill ran through her body, only matched by the rush of battle. Forgetting they still stood in battle, Lars' hands roamed up Triska's back, setting her skin ablaze with lust. Slipping her hands under his shirt, Triska ran her fingers over the defined muscles of his stomach. Why was he so distracting? How could she feel this way about an enemy? Was it curiosity? She had only known the warmth of the Norse; perhaps the Viking could make her experience something new.

An arrow doused in flames whizzed past the pair breaking them out of their resolve and reminding them they still stood in the dead centre of a battlefield. Triska charged back into battle without looking back at him, slicing her way through the settlement, leaving Lars where he stood.

CHAPTER 4

THE BRITISH KNEW they had lost. With most of their men dead, the rest ran a swift retreat. Lars watched from afar as Triska rounded up the injured British troops for interrogation and gathered her wounded. She commanded the field with grace and authority; Lars was amazed by her. He quickly realised that his admiration for her was growing. He could still taste her on his tongue. Strolling through the battlefield, Lars wondered what he could say to regain her attention.

"Your people fight well. It leaves a lot to be admired," Lars offered an olive branch.

Triska turned to him. The lust in her eyes from their kiss was long gone, fury now in its place. Sheathing her weapons, she made her way swiftly to him, jamming a fist into his chest.

"This is *your* doing. You led them here; they only came because they wanted *you*!" she barked, alerting everyone nearby.

"I warned you war was coming," Lars retorted.

"Your war! Not mine! Look around you! Look at my home. My people bleed because of you!" Triska roared.

"Triska, please," Gunnar approached. "When the British captured me, I got information from them. They were coming here whether Lars was here or not," Gunnar tried to reason with her.

Triska shot Gunnar a look to step down. She was displeased that her spy was speaking for her enemy.

"Should I blame you then? We could have been prepared if you had come here instead of going to our enemies. Count yourself lucky that we have no dead, or their blood would be on your hands!" Triska snapped, making Gunnar back down instantly.

Triska surveyed the damage. A few huts had taken a hit, but nothing so severe it couldn't be quickly repaired. The central courtyard was trashed, and the bodies of the enemies lay scattered around; the soil ran red with their blood. The Norsemen had quickly taken care of the British. A few of their own would need the attention of the healers for their wounds, but most of the injuries were superficial.

"I do not like repeating myself, so listen clearly. The British have never been our burden. This is an isolated incident brought here by you. We handled the British with ease. If they come back, we will deal with them again...and then, I'm sending them to your door," Triska jabbed Lars hard in the shoulder, waiting for his response, but none came.

Lars knew she was angry and hurt from the attack on her home. He would likely feel the same in her shoes, but Lars also knew women. There would be nothing he could offer to change her mind.

"You came here for help, and now I refuse. Leave my settlement while I still allow you to carry your head on your shoulders," Triska snarled before heading off towards her hut.

Triska stood at the entrance to her hut, watching, waiting for them to leave. Her stare was enough to make a man think of death. She watched as Lars, Laga, and Gunnar gathered their horses and left. Gunnar had made his choice. His side was now with the Vikings, a decision she would not forget in a hurry.

When the group was out of sight, Triska finally went inside to find her second in command, Velika, waiting. Velika and Triska had been friends for years. Friendship aside, Triska admired Velika's strategic and analytical mind. She had proven her worth as co-council many times over, and Triska looked forward to hearing her opinion on the matter.

"Care to speak your mind? I haven't seen you pace so aimlessly in years," Velika said, offering Triska a flagon of mead. Triska accepted the cup but didn't drink. She needed a clear head, and mead would only cloud her thoughts.

"What is there to speak of?" Triska asked, pacing back and forth.

"You may not like my words, but an alliance might be wise," Velika ventured.

Triska shot her a look of annoyance. How could she side with the Danes after they brought the British to their door? They were now stuck in a war that was not theirs to fight.

"Care to explain?" Triska snapped, slamming her drink on the small wooden table, spilling the contents.

"We won this battle. But if what Gunnar speaks is true, and war is coming, we do not stand a chance against the British army. The Vikings have two settlements that we know of, which means if we combine our forces, we stand a chance. We are outnumbered by the British. How do you think the King will fare if he hears of the fall of our first settlement? Under your guidance, no less."

Triska knew that Velika had a point, but that didn't mean she liked it. Even with Triska being one of the few female leaders favoured by her King, getting his approval for her to run the first settlement had still been a battle. The British may not have considered the Norse a threat due to their ill numbers, and Lars was right. Viking or Norseman, all the British saw were rising invader numbers on their shores.

"And how do you think the King would fare if he found out we sided with our enemy?" Triska challenged.

"In light of the situation and a growing threat, I think the King would find your choice in forming an alliance as judgement well placed."

Triska turned to unhook her belt and placed her swords in

the corner. Velika was right. But Triska couldn't get past the fact that the Brits had only turned up when Lars did. As her mind drifted over the battle, she couldn't stop thinking about how his muscles bulged as he fought, how his hand had felt on her arm, and how his lips had tasted. Triska's fingertips tingled with the thought of running them over his abs. She wondered if the rest of him was as solid. Shaking off the thought, she turned her attention back to Velika.

"Siding with the Vikings is one thing. But I do not trust Lars. There is something about him…."

"What? That he is a good fighter? That he didn't back down under your scrutiny? Or the fact that you grow feelings for him…." Velika asked with a smirk.

"Feelings? I do not know the man," Triska shot back defensively.

"Tris, I saw how you looked at him like you eyed Burka. May the gods care for his soul. You have looked at no man that way in years."

"My eyes fell on someone new, that is all," Triska scoffed.

CHAPTER 5

SLEEP DIDN'T COME easy for Triska that night. She tossed and turned in her cot. Her body was wracked with sweat, and her mind woke her body up to new longings.

His hands brushed against her skin. His lips caressed her neck. Her hands traced each of his muscles. She could feel her thighs wrapped tightly around his hips. She could taste his breath on her tongue – his fingers in her hair. Breathing came in quick short breaths; she could almost feel his body weighing down on hers.

"Triska," his voice whispered in her ear.

"Lars," she responded.

He took her breast in his mouth, teasing her aching nipples with each flick of his tongue.

"I need more, Lars," Triska ordered.

Obeying her command, Lars ran kisses down her stomach, hips, and thighs. Slowly, he pushed open her legs, his head moving into position. She could feel his breath at her opening.

Triska gasped, jumping up from her dream. Her body was soaked in a cold sweat, her heart racing. It had felt so real. She could almost feel his hands on her skin. Why was he occupying her thoughts so? Was she frustrated because her dream was of him? Or because he had neglected to finish his task, leaving her with an aching between her thighs that screamed for his attention.

Triska tried to get back to sleep, but her mind flashed with images from her dream. The more she remembered, the more her body ached to be touched. Finally, she decided to give in to her urges. Slipping her night dress off her shoulders, she lay back and closed her eyes. Images of Lars flashed in her mind as she ran her fingers over her skin, imagining her hands were his.

Her hands traced her breasts. She took her nipple between her fingers and began to tease it as her other hand traced the lines of her hips. Her fingers caressed her inner thighs as she dreamed of Lars' touch. Slipping her fingers between her legs, she gasped at the sensation. Gently, she caressed her aching bud. Triska bit her lip to keep her moans silent as she slipped her fingers inside.

Her hands were rich with her juices. She longed for Lars and imagined the things he could do to her body if the mere thought of him had her trembling. Her mind flashed with thoughts of their kiss, his tongue massaging hers as she increased her rhythm. Tension grew in the pit of her stomach, heat rising through her body like a wildfire. Licking her lips, she remembered his taste, inhaling. She recalled his rugged masculine scent.

Triska convulsed, her back arching as she reached climax. Relaxing back into her bed, Triska sighed in frustration. She had never had a problem pleasing herself before. It always soothed her. But this time was different. She needed more. She needed to feel Lars inside of her.

Frustrated with thoughts of the man that enraged her, Triska quickly dressed, deciding that if self-pleasing wouldn't satisfy her and sleep would not come, perhaps a walk in the night air would calm her down.

Wrapping her furs tight, she strolled, observing how the camp slept peacefully. The only sounds were that of nature and the night. The gentle rustle of the night air brushed through the trees. She could hear the faint buzzing of insects and the distant sound of waves lapping up against the shore.

She could hear the horses and moved closer to the walls of the camp. A shadow on the hill outside of camp caught her attention. The shadow moved closer to the camp walls. Triska was aware that she had ventured out unarmed but knew herself well enough that even a tiny rock could be an adequate weapon.

Slowly, she ventured towards the shadow, creeping around huts to cut whoever it was before they could raise the alarm, should there be others nearby. Sneaking out of the shadows, she met the one person she was not expecting to see. Lars.

It was late, and he was alone. Triska knew she should ask questions. Was he spying? Planning an attack of his own to rile the troops? Or had he come back for her.

"What are you doing here?" she asked.

"I was scouting the area, making sure no more troops lingered nearby," Lars whispered.

"Are you alone?" she asked.

"Of course," Lars answered.

With him standing in front of her in actual form, no longer a dream, her body came alive. She needed him closer to soothe her, to calm the ever-growing ache inside her. Lars looked back at her, confused by her silence.

With a glance to be sure she wasn't being followed, Triska slammed Lars against the wall, pinning him against the wood.

"What?..." Lars began.

Before he could utter any words to break her focus, Triska grabbed his hair and kissed him with the passion she longed for.

CHAPTER 6

LARS HAD TRAVELLED BACK to the Norse settlement to have words with Triska. He was still angry with her that she had turned him away. Not only that but without giving his argument proper thought after they had fought side by side.

On his travels back to the settlement, he had worked out a speech in his head, fighting his case once more. But since she had found him in the darkness, all sense had left his mind. She no longer wore the battle-ready leather armour she had earlier. She was dressed simply in a wool slip wrapped in furs to guard against the cold.

Lars was rendered speechless. Even with only the light of the moon around them, he could see the curves of her hips, her large breasts sitting proudly on her chest. Her legs were as strong as his, and he wondered what they would feel like wrapped around his waist.

She kissed him harder, pulling at his hair as if she couldn't get close enough to him. Lars knew it was probably not a good idea, but he could already feel himself growing at her touch.

"Trisk…" Lars began, but Triska pushed her fingers to his lips, silencing him.

Silently Triska began to undress Lars, pulling him free from the binds of his clothes. Unclipping her furs, she lay them on the ground at her feet, proceeding to remove her slip over her head. Lars stood, his jaw clenched tight. He wanted to let his jaw fall free. The sight of her was magnificent.

"Are you?..." But once again, Triska placed a finger to his lips.

Triska wrapped her hand around his jaw, kissing him, nipping at his bottom lip, and stroking his tongue with hers. Her hand retraced the muscles of his stomach before she found what she sought. Wrapping her fingers around his thick, hard cock, she slowly stroked him. He was enjoyably large, and she teased him the way he had in her dream. Lars gasped in the back of his throat.

Lars' hands ran down her back, caressing the curve of her hips before gripping her plump rear and lifting her up. She responded in kind, wrapping her legs tightly around him. Gently, Lars lowered her onto the furs.

"Triska…"

"Stop talking and just take me," Triska interrupted.

Lars didn't need to be told twice. With her laying beneath him, he pushed her legs wide. Stroking her entrance, he was pleased to find she was already wet, willing and ready for him. Lars slid himself inside her, letting out a small moan at the feel of her. She was so tight, gripping him with a force that threatened to send him over the edge too soon.

Lars pushed into her hard, smiling to himself as Triska's head fell back. A gasp escaped her lips, and her eyes closed as her hands clawed at his back. Her legs wrapped back around his waist, holding him close, not letting him go. Lars took hold of her breast, sucking her nipple between his teeth, stroking it with the tip of his tongue as he thrust harder and faster.

Triska's nails grazed the skin of his back, and her soft, gentle moans, barely a whisper, tickled his ear. As his pleasure grew, Triska began to grind her hips, matching his thrusts with her own. He could feel her tightening herself around him. The feeling was maddening.

Hooking an arm under her leg, Lars brought her leg up to

rest on his shoulder, allowing him to thrust deeper. Triska bit her lip, fighting to keep quiet. Lars longed to hear her moan her pleasure, but for now, the ecstasy on her face and the feeling of her body responding to him was enough. His thrusts increased as pleasure took over him, spilling himself inside her. Lars heard her gasp and felt her body shake beneath him as they climaxed together.

Lars panted, laying still above her, regaining himself for a while. Triska made no effort to move him. Finally, Triska pushed Lars away, gathered her clothes and swiftly redressed. Lars watched, confused.

"Triska..."

Again, her fingers met his lips, this time with a soft shake of the head. Lars pulled his clothes back on as quickly as he could as Triska vanished into the night. What had just happened? Where was she going? As soon as he could, Lars made his way to follow her. Eventually, he caught up to her close to her hut. She heard him coming and spun to face him. Her face was cold and stony.

"Do not follow me," she ordered, freezing Lars to the spot as she turned and left.

CHAPTER 7

THE FOLLOWING DAY, Triska woke feeling satisfied. Lars had not disappointed her. But now, she knew he would probably be waiting to talk with her. There was nothing more to say. The Brits were still an issue, and he was a distraction she no longer needed.

Calling for Velika, she summoned Gunnar and Lars.

"They left camp on your orders yesterday," Velika said, confused.

"They are not far out of camp. Send scouts to fetch them and bring them to me," Triska ordered.

Dressing quickly in her battle armour, she sat in her hut waiting patiently. Sure enough, it wasn't long before Velika and her scouts returned with Gunnar and Lars in tow.

"The fact my scouts found you so easily tells me you ignored my instruction. The Brit's attack will not be the last, and my people must prepare. Take your leave and return home," Triska said, keeping her face stern and her eyes on Lars.

Lars stood with a look of bewilderment.

"May I speak with you alone, Triska?" Lars asked, folding his arms across his chest.

Triska looked to Velika and nodded. Once the others had left,

Lars and Triska stayed in silence. She waited for him to speak, and Lars clearly wanted her to explain.

"You are not going to offer aid in the war?" Lars asked.

"I have said no. My word is final. I request that you leave."

"Why?" Lars asked.

"As I have said, my people need to prepare. I can't do that with you still here. Besides, it will not be long before the British make for your settlement. I'm merely offering you a courtesy head start."

Lars raised an eyebrow and muttered something that didn't reach Triska's ears. Shaking his head, he dropped his arms and stepped towards her. Instinctually, Triska rested her hand on the hilt of her sword.

"What if the British come back? Do you think they will go easy on you after their defeat? You are allowing your feelings for me to cloud your judgement," Lars stated.

"I have no feelings for you," Triska said coldly.

Lars took a step back, not believing the words coming from her lips. How could she say that? Lars might not know much about love, but he was not blind. The memory of her body reacting to him last night was still fresh.

"If you have no feelings, how do you explain the kiss on the battlefield? I may have initiated it, but you kissed me back. And what about last night?"

"You Vikings and your egos, thinking you are a gift sent from the gods for us women to enjoy."

"You can't tell me last night didn't mean anything," Lars insisted, trying to keep the hurt from his voice.

"Come on, Lars, we are not children. You Vikings brag about your conquests all the time. I simply made you one of mine," Triska shrugged.

Lars shook his head, running a hand through his hair. This was not the same woman from the last few days, was it? She may have been a strong leader, determined and proud, but he never considered her cold.

"Look me in the eye and tell me there is nothing between us, and I shall honour your request and leave," Lars said, staring deep into her eyes.

Triska sat unmoved by his words. Her face was as still as stone.

"I have no idea what you are talking about," she replied.

Lars looked back, waiting for the moment she would crack and say it was all a lie. But nothing changed.

"Then I shall take my leave."

CHAPTER 8

LARS DIDN'T WAIT AROUND to see if Triska changed her mind. He couldn't understand how she was being so stubborn or how she could ignore the spark between them. But, putting his hurt feelings aside, his mind was still focused on what to do about the impending British attack. Lars believed they could stand a chance between the settlement at the Point and the settlement run by the Jürgensen brothers. A little helping hand from the Norsemen wouldn't have gone a miss, though.

One of Triska's advisors, Irmusta, promised to ride with them to the halfway point. Lars was grateful for the gesture but felt that Triska had assigned yet another spy to make sure they left camp.

Gunnar, Irmusta, and Laga chatted amongst themselves. Lars was too busy stewing in his thoughts to engage. Replaying Triska's words made his blood boil. Every time he closed his eyes, he was faced with that hard stony look. Nothing Lars could say or do would change her mind. How was he going to explain this to the King? How were they going to fair against the British? Grumbling to himself, Lars worried he might go crazy.

"I am sorry, brother. Triska is known to be stubborn, but I thought she would listen," Gunnar said.

Lars grumbled an inaudible reply, his gaze glaring off into the distance.

"She has fought hard to prove herself a worthy leader. And so far, it has faired well. But, unfortunately, I feel the British attack didn't work in your favour," Irmusta spoke softly.

Lars grumbled again, his anger festering beneath the surface, threatening to come out at any moment.

"I have failed you. I have failed Laga. I know this to be true. I will not rest until I have done everything possible to help in this war," Gunnar said, finally sparking Lars' attention.

Looking over at his brother-in-law, he could see the sorrow and regret on his face as clear as the trees on the horizon. Yes, Lars was angry, but his anger was not at Gunnar.

"Do not apologise, Gunnar. You did not fail us. You came back when danger was imminent to warn us. You took an enemy of your leader into camp and vouched for them for a greater cause. My anger is not with you," Lars sighed deeply.

"I thought what you did was honourable. First, you came offering aid in a war we knew nothing about. Then, when our leader turned you down, you stayed to fight with us. I saw you on the battlefield. You have skill; it is much to be admired," Irmusta said.

"I don't understand how Triska could say no after such an attack," Laga finally spoke.

"The hatred between our people goes back far and runs deep. It is a hard thing to get past," Lars admitted.

Stewing in his thoughts and thinking over the last few days, Lars realised how much he had come to respect Gunnar. Not only did he come to offer aid, but he could also have sided with his leader. But instead, he rides back to the Point with them. While Lars initially thought Irmusta to be a spy, the more they talked, the more Lars realised that not everyone thought like Triska. Not everyone was ruled by blind anger and hatred. Perhaps an alliance would be possible. Maybe it was time to put old grudges aside and unite their people. The question was, how?

"Gunnar, you and Irmusta have opened my eyes. Perhaps one day, our people can soon get past our dark history and learn to live in peace. Not everyone is so clouded by the past. Perhaps we should all take a leaf from the book of the young. Your minds are far more advanced than that of an old fool like me," Lars said.

"Are you saying that you think an alliance is possible?" Laga asked.

"Maybe one day," Lars answered after a moment's thought.

The sun descended over the hills, basking the distant shoreline in warm, soft hews of orange. They would reach the halfway point soon, but as night crept in, they agreed making camp for the night would be the best option.

Irmusta made the fire while Gunnar went out hunting for food. Laga prepared camp, and Lars watched for any sign of approaching enemies. As the last rays of light from the day vanished and the moon rose high in the sky, talk returned to what it would take to get Triska to agree to an alliance.

Laga skinned the rabbits and placed them on the fire. The smell was delicious, making everyone's mouths water in anticipation. None had realised just how hungry they were.

"I mean no ill will with my words, but Triska isn't the only Norse leader. If she does not agree to an alliance, perhaps someone else will," Laga said.

"I love your fire, Laga, but Triska's settlement is the only Norse one on these shores. For now," Gunnar smiled, wrapping his arms around his wife.

"For now," Irmusta grinned, causing Gunnar to jab her playfully in the arm.

They ate their food and talked around the warmth of the campfire. Irmusta told stories of her lost love, and Laga and Gunnar shared their dreams for their life together. All the while, Lars couldn't get Triska off his mind. She had him perplexed.

Lars admired her determination to protect her people. Her leadership and drive were remarkable. Her skills with a sword were wildly impressive, and her body was like something carved out by the gods. She was everything he ever thought he wanted in a woman, yet she had tossed him aside. A longing, aching in his chest, left Lars unsettled; what was this feeling? What had Triska done to him? Lars needed time alone to process his thoughts.

"I shall take my leave and get some rest. Sleep well, my friends," Lars bid everyone good night.

Strolling over to the edge of the camp, Lars prepared to sleep when he looked back towards the Norse settlement. Night had gathered around them. But there was enough light in the sky to illuminate the sight; and no mistake in what he saw. Billowing through the trees were clouds of thick black smoke. Immediately, his mind raced to Triska as his heart constricted in his chest.

There was far too much smoke for it to be from campfires. The settlement was under attack. She needed him whether she wanted his help or not, and Lars wasn't going to sit around and do nothing. Jumping to his feet, he charged back towards camp.

"What's wrong?" Laga asked in a panic.

"Fire. The settlement has been attacked; we must go back," Lars answered, readying his horse.

"I will ride with you. Irmusta, take Laga the rest of the way to the Point and warn the others," Gunnar prepared his horse.

"I don't think so; I ride with you!" Laga argued.

"We do not have time for arguing. Laga, do not engage unless you have to. Stay to the outer edges of the settlement. Hide in the trees if you must. But nothing will be left to save if we do not get back soon," Lars ordered.

Not waiting to see what the others did or hear any more of their words, Lars climbed on his horse and galloped off towards Triska.

CHAPTER 9

THE ENTIRE SETTLEMENT stood in flames. Lars didn't feel close enough no matter how hard he tried. The British had arrived again with double the force. Gunnar and Irmusta charged close behind. The Norse were strong warriors, but with the size of the British troops, Lars feared they didn't stand a chance.

"Take out as many as you can! I'm going to find Triska," Lars ordered, leaping from his horse and making his way through the fight.

The Norse fought at odds three to one; the battle looked like it had already been lost. Dead from both sides littered the battlefield. With eyes blazing red with anger, Lars barged through the fight, swinging his axe to take down solider after solider.

The flames roared as they spread from hut to hut. Men caught by the fire screamed in pain, and dying gasps filled the air. If this was the first sign of war, Lars feared that if an alliance wasn't formed soon, both Norse and Vikings would perish.

Lars brandished his axe like never before, cleaving heads and breaking necks. While he fought off two troops, a sword almost pierced his back, only to be stopped by the duel-wielding hands of Triska. Lars felt he could breathe for the first time since re-entering the settlement. Triska was alive. Covered in the blood of the dead, with a deep cut to her shoulder Triska didn't let that stop her. Silently, they fought side by side.

Lars tossed his axe through the flaming battlefield stopping an attack that could have rendered his sister a widow. Gunnar looked back, offering Lars a nod of thanks before running his sword through the gut of another soldier.

"Lars!" Triska yelled, tossing him one of her swords.

Lars was impressed by the weight of the sword, even more impressed with how Triska had handled it with ease. Velika appeared from the flames with a burn covering her arm as she fought to guard the young, helping them flee the settlement. Seeing her second in danger, Triska ran for the troop; grabbing the back of his cloak, she ripped him away. Lars grabbed the soldier before he could regain his footing, spearing Triska's sword through his back before tossing him into the burning remains of the nearest hut.

The battle raged on with screams of the defenceless as they were set upon; battle cries and metal hitting metal. The settlement crumbled around them as the flames devoured everything they touched. This wasn't just a simple attack or a warning; this was a declaration of war and the horrors to come.

The British soldiers had been well trained, giving Lars and the Norse a fight to remember. The soldiers had come prepared with shields to guard against attack. But Lars and Triska held the anger of generations and broke through their shields, fighting to claim victory.

With a break in the fight, Lars took a second to scan his surroundings; the end of the battle was near. A roar from behind alerted Lars to yet another attack. A soldier matching his height and build charged at him, sword in hand. Raising his sword, Lars blocked the attack, shoving his boot into the man's gut and knocking him backwards. Not giving the man a second to recover, Lars lunged, but his sword met the man's shield.

Lars struggled as the man fought with as much ferociousness and power as three men. Anger burned in Lars' chest. Roaring,

Lars swung his sword and buried it in the man's shield. Using the move to his advantage, the soldier twisted his shield and tossed it aside, taking Lars' sword with it and leaving him unarmed. Lars leapt back, twisting to the side. Lars kicked out, swiping the man's legs from under him. Triska appeared just in time to bury her sword in the soldier's back before he could recover and attack again.

"Thank you," Lars offered.

"Don't thank me yet. The battle is not over," Triska said before running off to help the others.

The battle raged through most of the night. Finally, the last of the British troops fell to the Norse by sunrise. It was a long battle with plenty of losses on both sides. The Norse had won, but just barely.

Lars, Gunnar, Triska, Velika, and Irmusta gathered in the centre of what remained of the settlement. Triska barked orders to the few remaining men to douse the flames and save whatever they could.

"There is not much left to save. I suggest we regroup at the Point," Lars said, grabbing Triska's arm, hoping to make her see sense.

"I am not leaving my home," Triska barked, pulling her arm free.

"We will claim this land back...."

"I am *not* yielding this land. This is our land; they will not take it from me again!" Triska yelled.

"Look around, Triska! The battle is already lost. Look at what remains of your people. If the British come back, you will not stand a chance. If you lose, we all lose. Both Norse and Dane cannot afford for the British to get another foothold in the North. So come with me. And when we return, we shall return with a force that will make the British tremble in their boots. We will reclaim this land and rebuild stronger than before."

Lars waited for Triska's answer. He could see the pain and fear in her eyes. She turned to Velika for guidance. Lars knew that look; it was one he had held himself. Triska questioned herself, was she making the right choice?

"Are you proposing an alliance?" Triska asked.

"Since the moment I got here," Lars answered.

Triska took a moment. Sizing him up, debating with herself if she could trust him or not. Then, sighing deeply, she offered out her hand.

"Fine, an alliance it shall be. But I want to have my say over what resources we use; this is my settlement, after all. So, Velika, I leave you in charge. I shall travel to the Point with you, Lars," Triska nodded, a small smile touching the edge of her lips.

CHAPTER 10

TRISKA SAT PROUDLY on her horse as she rode into the Point with Lars, Gunnar, and the others. She pretended she didn't see the angry looks and hands grabbing at hilts. She couldn't blame them for being defensive. She acted the same when Lars ventured into her camp.

"Prepare for war!" Lars ordered.

Triska admired the way Lars' men respected his command. No one stopped to question who the war was with or the fact he rode in with the leader of the Norse settlement. Instead, men clambered to the settlement walls bracing them for an attack; archers climbed to the defences while others went to gather supplies.

"What are my orders?" a man Triska later found out was named Birgen asked.

"Ready the ships," Lars commanded.

Birgen called for his men and headed for the shore. Triska could see Lars was in his element. He was made for command. Sword maidens armed themselves, and the blacksmith was hot on everyone's tails handing out new weaponry. Lars barked command after command but jumped in to help barricade walls. Triska couldn't help but admire him and questioned if she had misjudged him. Nagging in her mind, she thought she should have put her pride aside and listened to him sooner.

Being the strong, proud leader she was, it was hard for Triska to admit that sometimes she needed guidance. But watching Lars, she felt she had found her equal.

"Your people respect your lead. It's an admirable trait. Dare I say I regard you as my equal?" Triska blushed, finally letting her feelings shine through.

"I hold you to the same regard," Lars grinned.

"I fear I may have wounded you with how I acted after that night outside the camp walls," Triska dropped her gaze, unable to meet Lars' eyes.

Lars gently raised her chin, forcing her to look at him.

"It matters not. I can see your true feelings in those eyes," Lars smiled.

"We both run our own settlements; how are we supposed to…." Lars stopped her with a brief soft kiss.

"We will figure out how to be together…after the war," Lars smiled.

The world around them was falling into chaos. War had been a mere whisper in the night, but now it approached with the fury of a thousand fires. Yet, through all the madness, all Lars knew was that with Triska, everything made sense. He had a beautiful, strong woman who knew her mind and wasn't afraid to speak it. She was loyal to her people and a successful leader who commanded and received respect. She was the female version of him.

"Triska, before war bridges our doorstep, I need to speak my truth. Your words did not wound me. On the contrary, the thought of you falling to the British with me not being by your side wounded me," Lars said low enough for only Triska to hear.

"Careful, Dane, or I may think you hold feelings for me," Triska smiled.

"I do not claim to know much of love. But when I rode

towards the flames, my heart felt like it was burning too. The thought of losing you was too much to bear," Lars admitted.

"What else could that be but love?" Triska asked.

"My thoughts exactly," Lars grinned, pulling Triska into his arms.

The Vikings prepared for battle, guarding the walls and yelling commands to one another. But while they were in each other's arms, they wouldn't have noticed if the whole world had been on fire. Lars stroked Triska's cheek, memorising her face as if it were the last time he would see it. Triska pulled Lars closer, pressing her lips to his.

EPILOGUE

THE SETTLEMENT LAY in silent wait. The women and children had been evacuated to neighbouring villages with a small guard in case the British dared to venture their way. The walls had been reinforced, and archers guarded the walls. The horses were all saddled and prepared. Barricades and trenches had been dug outside the settlement walls, and the ships were manned, ready to set sail. Scouts and messengers had been sent to the other settlement, with their riders galloping through the night.

Lars, Birgen, Gunnar, Triska, Irmusta, and the rest of Lars' war council gathered inside. Debates had raged through the night. The main point of discussion was how many ships should be sent out.

"The British have already shown great force. We do not want to leave our numbers short by sending too many out on the ships. Their ships are no match for ours. We need enough ships to guard from the sea and one to reach the other settlement; three ships should be enough," Triska offered.

She had seen the force of the British. She had suffered too many losses to risk underestimating them again. Lars knew her words held sense but convincing the others would be a task.

"We are strongest at sea; we can cover a vaster area and attack before they reach us. Therefore, the more ships, the better," Birgen argued.

"Don't be foolish. If all our men are at sea, who will defend the walls? What if they set the settlement ablaze like they did with the Norse? There will not be enough hands to douse the flames," a grey-haired Viking argued.

"How about splitting our forces in half? Half by sea, half on land?" Gunnar asked.

"These are not your forces to command," someone snapped.

"Enough! We have a common enemy. An alliance has been formed. Their forces are our forces, and ours are theirs the same!" Lars' voice boomed, silencing the room.

So many voices and minds had the argument raging until a compromise was finally met. Three ships would span the coast, and two would try and reach the first settlement. Tired from arguing, everyone ventured to bed. They needed rest for the battle to come.

Triska waited outside the castle's great hall while Lars bid goodnight to his men. Then, spotting her waiting, Lars strolled over to her, still muttering to himself. They had talked enough for one night; Triska had other things on her mind.

Grabbing him, she pushed him against the wall silencing him with a kiss as passionate as their first on the battlefield.

"Do we still need to discuss the war plans, or can you not think of a better way to spend the night?" Triska smirked, pulling at Lars' waistband.

"I would much rather spend my evening discussing strategy with you," Lars grinned.

"Strategy? We can finalise the details for the war in the morning. Right now, I would rather silence your mind and put that mouth of yours to more entertaining uses."

Finally understanding her meaning, Lars' eyes darkened, filled with lust and hunger. Taking his hand, Triska led him to the room she had been assigned for the duration of her stay. It was a quaint room once used by Ailsa's mother. Small enough to be comfortable yet with enough room for the two of them to make use of. A small cot lay against the far wall close to a small stone fireplace. The dimming ambers of the fire flickered slowly. Trinkets and decorations littered the shelves, and a small wooden table big enough for two with a single chair sat in the middle of the room.

Triska had been working on a few battle plans of her own. Her battle plans were still laid out on the table. Lars headed over to the table, scanning over her plans; they were good, brilliant. She had drawn out a planned attack on all fronts, men hidden along the trail leading to the Point; ships guarding from the sea, and drawings of larger crossbows that could bridge more ground than their standard archers. She had trails of fire to trap the enemy. Triska was remarkable.

"Your battle plans are astonishing. Why didn't you present them to the council?" Lars asked.

Triska swept the plans off the table, sending scrolls, wooden carvings, and runes scattering across the floor. She placed her finger to his lips and sat on the table before him.

"I told you, no more battle talk tonight," Triska whispered. "Put that smart mouth of yours to better use."

Lars pressed a soft kiss against her finger and watched as Triska unhooked her armour. Lars began to unhook his furs and pulled his tunic over his head. Then, pushing Triska's skirts high up her thighs, he pushed her legs apart, thrusting himself between her thighs. Triska ran her hands over Lars' solid chest, letting her head fall back as Lars ran his fingers up her back, entwining his fingers in her hair.

"Triska, you are magnificent. A warrior to be envied. Your mind is as beautiful as your body. Why hide your talents? Your plans should be presented to the council," Lars breathed into her ear, nipping at her earlobe and trailing kisses down her neck.

"Your admiration is well appreciated, Lars. But I am a Norse leader in your camp. I must get your people to trust me first. I would be called a fool coming in and barking orders," Triska moaned.

"I will kill anyone who dares speak ill of you," Lars growled, his lips trailing down her collar bone to her breasts.

"You would, wouldn't you?" Triska smiled.

"I would burn them all for you," Lars growled, his hands pawing at her breasts, taking each nipple in turn, making Triska moan louder.

"My Dane," Triska breathed, pulling his face up to hers.

Triska hooked her legs tight around his hips, pulling him closer. She kissed him deeply, her tongue tasting his words.

"I would do anything for you," Lars growled.

"Then take me like the warrior you are," Triska moaned in his ear.

Lars unhooked himself from Triska's grasp, pushing her down so she lay flat against the table. Lars dropped to his knees, and spread Triska's legs open wide. Triska rested back, running her fingers through Lars' thick dark hair. Triska could feel Lars' breath warming her inner thighs; closing her eyes, she remembered her dream.

Lars trailed kisses upwards until his mouth began to explore the part of her that ached for his touch. Triska let out a moan of pleasure as his tongue lapped over her aching bud. As his tongue worked its magic, his fingers spread her lips apart and stretched her wide. Triska's hands explored her breasts, stroking and pinching her aching nipples. Her breathing quickened as he brought her closer and closer to the ecstasy she craved. Triska moaned louder as her pleasure grew, only for Lars to stop.

Before Triska could question him, Lars grabbed her hips and pulled her off the table. Flipping her around, he lay her flat and wrapped her braids around his hand, making her arch her back. Lars ran his hand over her buttocks, stroking the round plump flesh before swatting at her. Then, guiding himself to her entrance, he thrust deep inside her.

"Lars, my Dane," Triska groaned.

Lars pounded Triska harder, the sound of their bodies colliding and their panting breath filling the room. Triska clenched herself around him, releasing him only to squeeze herself again. From his moans, Triska knew it was driving Lars crazy.

Lars felt his pleasure building but wanted to see Triska's face as they arrived together. Pulling himself free, Lars flipped Triska around, placing her on the table's edge.

"Grip the table, support yourself," Lars growled as he hooked his arms under her knees, resting her legs high on his shoulders.

Triska obeyed his order and gasped as he entered her again. Triska's breasts bounced on her chest under Lars' punishing rhythm. Then, reaching his hand between her legs, Lars circled the sweet bud with his thumb, relishing in Triska's trembles.

"By the gods, Lars," Triska cried.

"Look at me, Triska, keep those beautiful eyes on me," Lars ordered.

Triska locked eyes with Lars as he pounded faster, harder, stroking her bud in a tantalising rhythm. Their moans of ecstasy grew until both were gasping for breath. She could feel her climax brewing deep inside, but she didn't want to feel her release until he reached his. Instead, she wanted to feel his release inside her, to feel the mighty warrior claim his victory.

"Lars!" Triska cried out.

"Triska!" Lars matched her cry as his release took over.

Triska finally allowed herself to feel her release, squeezing herself around him feeling every inch. Lars scooped her into his arms and carried her across to the cot. Laying her down, he pulled her close to his chest, kissing her forehead gently.

"Now, do you wish to talk battle plans?" Lars chuckled.

"I'd rather do that again," Triska growled, climbing on top of him, claiming her own victory.

THE END

Did you enjoy the Lars and Triska's story?
Please review it on <u>Goodreads</u>, or <u>Bookbub.</u>

STEN

FORGIVEN BY THE WARRIOR

PROLOGUE

STEN WAS MORE amazed than anyone when Ulster returned to the settlement. No one wanted him there. The entire settlement had practically cheered when the British captured him. Ulster mumbled madly about his time in the camp but wouldn't talk about what happened, other than when they realised he was of no use, they planned to kill him. But Ulster was slippery. And it was no surprise to Sten that he had managed to escape. The biggest shock was that his older brother now stood battered and bruised, arguing with him about leaving.

"I am your *brother*, Sten. Family! Blood! I have been made a fool of, an outcast and then left for dead at the hands of the British. We are leaving for Norway tonight!" Ulster barked.

Sten was sick of being ordered around by his brother. He wasn't a boy anymore; he was a man and didn't need to be told what to do.

"You cannot tell me what to do, Ulster. I will not return with you," Sten argued.

Ulster stopped turning to face his brother with the same evil glare Sten remembered from childhood. Ulster's eyes had always been dark. But when he was blinded in his right eye, leaving it like the shadow of a ghost, his gaze became bone-chilling. Sten would not be bullied anymore. He had spent his life falling in line with his brother's orders. Now, he wanted something different. Independence. A life of his own.

Ulster towered over Sten, baring his teeth into a snarl like a rabid, blood-hungry animal. But Sten stood his ground. He would not be intimidated anymore. When he was younger, Sten had no choice but to do what his brother ordered out of fear. As Sten grew older, doing what Ulster wanted had just become the norm. Sten had always known Ulster to be a cruel, crass man and never wanted to be anything like him. Sten grew tired of living in his brother's shadow. It was a dark, lonely, and cold place. And Sten wished to bask in the sun.

"What did you say to me? I am your older brother. You will do as I say!" Ulster barked, spit landing on Sten's cheek as he did.

"I shall not! I am not a child anymore, Ulster. I will not bend to your will anymore. Go back to Norway without me. No one wants you here," Sten yelled back.

The two brothers stood nose to nose, neither backing down. Ulster had the height over Sten, but Sten was more robust and skilled with a sword, bow, and any other weapon he put his hand to. Ulster would never admit it, but if Sten decided to fight back, Ulster wouldn't stand a chance.

"What did you say?" Ulster growled.

"You are unwanted. Go home if you so wish; I am staying here," Sten answered.

"No one, huh? Does that include you, *brother*? You would betray your family by choosing these people over me?"

Ulster made every attempt to intimidate Sten, but it was evident to Sten that Ulster knew he had lost.

"Call it what you will, Ulster. I'm done. I chose to stay here, with or without you," Sten said, turning to leave his brother to pack up his one-person boat.

"You have no life here. You may think yourself an honourable man, but you are *my* brother. And we both know our people do not easily forgive. Do you think they will accept you? Ha! They will think no more of you than they do me. You think you can start here anew? No woman will ever want you. You are not half the man I am," Ulster let out an evil laugh grabbing his crotch, shaking himself vigorously, and laughing at Sten.

"Goodbye, brother. May I never have to cast eyes on you again," Sten snarled, turning away in disgust.

Even if Ulster's words held an ouch of truth, a life alone was better than a tortured life in his shadow. No more would Sten have to do as he was told like a petulant child. He was free.

CHAPTER 1

THE PROBLEM with new beginnings is not everyone is ready to offer a second chance. It seemed that people were not easy to rush to forgiveness on account of Ulster. Olga had noticed the handsome Norseman who arrived with the monster Ulster, and hadn't been able to pull her eyes away from him since. Sten was an enigma. But everyone treated him as if Ulster's crimes against Velika were his own. Yet he remained unphased and eager to help.

He was shorter than his brother but was visibly stronger. His hair was not an untamed mess upon his head like his brother's; it was cut short on the sides and left long on top. He had his hair braided down his back in a way Olga admired. Unlike Ulster, this man didn't hide his face behind his beard. He was clean-shaven, showing off an impressive jawline. His eyes were kind and warm, a deep brown Olga could get lost in.

But his looks weren't the thing that caught her attention. Why hadn't he left with his brother? Why stay behind and be at the mercy of everyone's scrutiny for crimes that were not his own? Family was important to Olga, with her being an only child. She couldn't understand how someone could leave blood behind so quickly, even if Ulster was despicable.

Olga watched for days after Ulster departed, keeping to the

shadows, keen not to let Sten spot her watching him. Olga noted how he was polite and introduced himself with respect and honour. She watched how he was spat at and ignored in return. It didn't take long to discover his name. Sten was a lot nicer than Ulster, Olga thought. Sten didn't let the ill words, side glances, or shoves out of the way get him down. If anything, it fueled him to try harder.

Olga was a good spy and was surprised to find that Sten was earnest, intelligent, and skilled in multiple things. He reacted to all the ill wishes like he was used to it, expecting it as if he deserved it. The thought concerned Olga, but she was smart enough not to judge others based on their actions; she preferred to get closer and combine their efforts with their character.

Olga stood grooming the horses, a good cover for observing. She watched as Sten busied himself with the livestock, not sticking around to receive thanks. When Olga returned to her hut, she was surprised to find all her jobs done. Sten had made himself useful without anyone even realising. It intrigued Olga. What was his plan? What was he up to? She couldn't figure out how he gained from doing this if no one knew it was he who completed the tasks.

Lars and Triska had returned, spending the day locked in the council hut with Gunnar, Velika, Birgen, and a few other members of the team. Olga made excuses not to be involved so she could watch Sten further.

"Olga, Triska, and Lars summon you," Birgen said, making Olga jump.

She had been so focused she hadn't heard him approach and hoped he hadn't noticed her startle. What kind of spy doesn't notice someone approaching from the rear?

"I shall be there in a moment," she said, watching as Birgen summoned a few others, including the Norseman Sten.

When Olga arrived at the council hut, it appeared a plan had already been formed. Triska and Velika chatted intently over the battle plans across the table. Looking around the room, Olga noticed the selection of people summoned. Both Norse and Dane, sword maidens, scouts, farmers, and warriors alike. Someone from every community who called the settlement home. With such a selection of varied skills, Olga wondered what they had planned.

"Thank you all for gathering so quickly," Triska said, silencing the muttering around the room.

"We have been discussing the recent attack and our victory," Velika said, making the room cheer.

Everyone was still feeling the adrenaline rush that came with victory and glory.

"We were prepared this time, but we still do not know what the British are planning. So we must be prepared rather than sitting and getting fat waiting for them. We need to take the war to them," Velika continued.

Heads around the room nodded in unison; everyone hung on her every word.

"I could not agree more. It has been decided that we need spies to infiltrate the British camp. So we have gathered you here today looking for volunteers...." Triska said.

Olga didn't hear the rest of Triska's speech. Nevertheless, she had heard what she needed to. Without letting Triska finish, Olga leapt to her feet, dimly aware by the scraping of a chair being pushed back that she was not the only one so eager to volunteer.

"I volunteer!" Olga yelled.

Curiosity pricked at her, causing the hairs on the back of her neck to stand on end. Then, turning around, her eyes grew wide. Standing at the back of the hut was the other volunteer. Sten.

CHAPTER 2

"HIM? I do not trust him. The blood of that *monster* runs through his veins. So, we cannot trust him," a voice yelled through the room.

Sten didn't know who voiced their concerns, nor did he care. This was not new to him. Guilt by association was to be expected. Not that Sten considered himself innocent. He may have chosen to look the other way to his brother's cruel ways out of self-protection. Or had it been that he just refused to see the extent of Ulster's cruelty? Had a part of him expected Ulster to have a good bone somewhere in his body? Or was it a young boy's foolish hope that the only male figure in his life saved his cruelty for him and him alone? It mattered not anymore; Ulster was gone.

But Sten was not that frightened boy anymore. He had fought back home in Norway to prove himself a warrior. He may have shared a ship with his brother, but most of the time, Sten kept to himself and only interacted with his brother when unavoidable. The true extent of Ulster's crimes had been unknown to Sten, or were they? Ever since Velika had outed Ulster, Sten had tortured himself thinking he should have seen the signs. Had they been there all along, and he missed them? He knew his brother was cruel; he had felt that first hand. Now,

Sten wanted to make up for his brother's misdeeds and prove they were not the same man.

"I am not my brother," Sten said calmly.

Sten was not interested in upsetting anyone but also wanted to make it clear to the settlement that he was his own person. Ulster had fled like the coward Sten knew him to be. Sten was good at odd jobs and had grown used to doing jobs no one else wanted to do to prove his worth. Now an opportunity had presented itself, giving him a new plan. He needed to be the hero. Volunteering for such a dangerous mission and coming back with helpful information could make him just that. It would raise him up to be someone to be respected.

The Danish sword maiden, known as Olga, who he had seen following him around camp had also volunteered. It was hard to miss her. She was gorgeous. The beauty of a queen in the shell of a warrior, what was not to love? Her hair fell around her shoulders in thick golden waves. She had high cheekbones with an angular jaw and eyes like a lioness, as blue as the new morning sky. If Sten had not seen her in battle with his own eyes, he would have thought her a delicate morning flower. But, instead, she had the power of a bear, the gracefulness as the cresting waves, and the anger of the sun. She was a contradiction in every form and completely mesmerising. But, even if she was a skilled warrior, to Sten, this was no mission for someone like her.

"I volunteered first. Allow the maiden to stay here and protect," Sten protested.

"Do not let my lack of a cock fool you, Norseman. My sword cuts as deep, my arrows fly as fast, and I have spilt more British blood than you. I have been on these shores longer; I should go."

"I do not question your skill; I merely suggest you may be too obvious as a spy. And I volunteered first!" Sten protested again.

"Too obvious as a spy? State your meaning!" Olga yelled.

Sten's lips fell silent, but his mind screamed *your beauty*.

CHAPTER 3

Olga protested further. Perhaps she had misjudged the Norseman too soon, and he wasn't the gentle soul she perceived him to be.

"Lars, you are my commander; say something!" Olga roared.

Triska and Lars stood heads together discussing the matter. Olga grew more agitated; it felt like her ability was being questioned. A sentiment she didn't like one bit.

"It appears an opportunity has presented itself. A way of strengthening our alliance. A member from each group may be wise," Lars spoke.

"Do not paint this as something it is not. I am mistrusted due to my brother. If anyone here trusted me, I would be doing this alone. I do not need a nursemaid!" Sten barked back.

His words only fueled Olga's newfound frustration with him. Nursemaid? Did he not whom he spoke about? She was anything but a nursemaid.

"I volunteered fair and square. I do not need a man to hold my hand. My history speaks for itself. I spied for the King himself. And I am certainly no nursemaid!" Olga roared, losing grip on her temper.

"Why else other than miss trust would the Danish spy want to ride with me?" Sten argued.

Olga needed this mission more than anyone knew. She had her own secret mission, close to her heart, that not even her brothers in arms had gotten word. She didn't like being questioned; it was no one's business but hers.

"I do not need to answer to the likes of you, Norseman," Olga spat.

"Enough petty squabbling!" Velika ordered. "I do not question your judgement, Lars, nor yours, Triska. Yet I do not truly know Olga or what lays in her heart. My mind would be at ease knowing a Norseman was with her."

Olga looked around the room for anyone to fight in her corner. She wasn't the type to need others' help or approval. But from the bowed heads and averted gazes, she knew she was alone on the matter. Lars and Triska didn't object. Velika's statement worked well for the alliance, no matter how she dressed it. Instead, the room grew with tension so thick that the air was suffocating.

Reluctantly, Olga turned to face Sten. To her surprise, he nodded. It was agreed. They would ride out together.

CHAPTER 4

LARS THOUGHT it best for Olga and Sten to don a disguise. It would be far too clear for the enemy to see them for who they were if they rode out in full battle armour. Triska arranged for the healers to crush petals and berries to mask Olga's blonde hair. She didn't have the rich auburn hair the Scottish ladies had, but it would suffice.

Riding out, Olga twisted in the constraints of her new clothing. There was nowhere for her to conceal her sword. Dressed as a farmer, Olga felt like a fool. She didn't like heading into enemy territory unarmed, so she tied two daggers to her thighs.

"We look ridiculous. Who will be stupid enough to think we are Scots?" Olga complained.

She wore a long-patterned wool dress over a simple cotton slip and wool skirt that was coarse against her skin. Her breasts sat high on her chest, framed by the delicate white trim of the slip beneath her clothes. She found the wool shawl around her shoulder a nuisance, restricting her movements and constantly slipping down her arms. Sten wore a simple grey tunic with rope acting as his belt and matching long draws beneath. He might have passed for a farmer if he were not so robust, but what farmer did Olga know who housed as much muscle as Sten?

"It is a good plan….and you do not look ridiculous. The dress suits you," Sten offered.

"Oh, shut up!" Olga snapped.

She was not in the mood to converse with the Norseman, no matter how pleasing he was to the eye. He may have held her attention before, but no longer. Now, he was just an obstacle in her way. Flattery would get him nowhere with her. How was she to enact her plan with a babysitter following her every move? She thought about telling him but didn't trust he wouldn't report her secret back to Lars and the others. Yet another reason for her to hate him.

"I mean no offence, Olga. I saw you on the battlefield when the British attacked. You wielded your sword better than some of my brothers' men," Sten said, trying to be friendly.

"Yet you thought to question my resolve in front of my commander and had the gall to insinuate I was a nursemaid," Olga snapped.

"A slip of the tongue in a moment of frustration. I meant no ill-will by it," he conceded.

"I would sooner cut your tongue from your mouth than hear you speak to me again," Olga snarled, spurring her horse further ahead.

"What is your problem with me? I have done nothing to wrong you!" Sten yelled after her, spurring his horse to catch up.

Olga's patience grew thin. Each word that slipped from Sten's lips vexed her more. His voice grated against her ears. She couldn't think clearly with his incessant yammering.

"You are in the way! A useless object blocking my mission. I would do better without you!" Olga barked, pulling her horse to a stop.

Olga glared at him, waiting for him to argue back. She was ready for a fight. She would lay him on his back and leave him to the wolves. He was wasting her time.

"Is it not enough my own people shun me for the acts of my

brother? So now you Danes do it too?" Sten asked, his brow furrowed deep down his nose.

"This has nothing to do with that creature with which you share blood. He understood when he was not wanted and left. Something you might think to do," Olga scoffed, pressing her horse forward, following the path through the woods.

"Unlike my brother, I am no coward, and I do not back down when I have given my word. Lars and Triska assigned us both to this mission. I am staying whether you like it or not," Sten yelled again, trying to keep up with her.

"Well, one thing we can agree on is I do not like you here," Olga grumbled.

"Here, or just me? You have no problem voicing your concerns, so speak them now. Better to air our grievances lest they interrupt our mission," Sten snapped, ducking as Olga let go of a tree branch that swung at his head.

"Grievances? What issue do you have with me?" Olga laughed.

"How about the fact I have done you no wrong, yet you seem to think so little of me."

"Oh, poor Norseman, does he need the approval of his nurse-maid?" Olga taunted.

"Do not mock me, Dane!" Sten boomed.

"Or what, Norseman?" Olga laughed again.

"Unlike my brother, I have never and will never raise my hand to a woman," Sten replied, only for Olga to return with a retort of her own.

"Then you must tremble in battle against a sword maiden like myself," Olga chided.

"Battle is different, and you know it. Why do you insist on acting like a child? Mocking me so?"

"Because I want you to leave me be!" Olga snapped.

"I will tell you what I said to my brother. I do not take orders from you! I am staying!"

"Then hold your irritating….," Olga stopped.

In the middle of the woods was the river they needed to cross. A small drawstring bridge shook in the breeze across the banks. Olga fell silent. The bridge did not look secure; the river waters ran furiously downhill and were too deep to risk pushing the horses through.

"What is it?" Sten asked, concerned.

"Nothing....we need to find another way across the river," Olga answered.

"Why? There is a bridge; come on," Sten said.

Olga's chest heaved. She swallowed to try and ease the lump in her throat.

"You look doubtful," Sten offered.

"That tiny thing will not hold the weight of the horses; we can't make the rest of the journey without them," Olga lied.

CHAPTER 5

"OLGA, it is alright to be concerned, but it is just water," Sten said softly.

He could tell she was scared but couldn't figure out why. They had gotten off on the wrong foot already. He didn't want to push her to talk about something she would not be willing to admit.

"I am concerned for the horses. Come, we shall find another way," Olga insisted, dismounting and leading her horse away.

Sten jumped from his horse and gently took her hand. Olga looked back at him in alarm, not out of fear but she was surprised at his gentle touch.

"I know you do not wish me to be here, but I am. You are not alone; I will help you cross, then I will come back and bring the horses," Sten offered kindly.

"The horses...."

"Olga, you are scared. I will tell no one. Please, allow me to help you across," Sten gently led her to the riverbank.

Sten could feel Olga's hand trembling in his. Her eyes darted from her foot on the bridge down to the river and back. Sten took her other hand. He placed it on the rope railing and held her other hand tightly, keeping a close eye on her, taking one slow step at a time. Sten offered gentle, soothing words as they walked, which seemed to ease her mind. Suddenly, a log raced down the river towards them. It smashed against the rocks below but did not touch the bridge. That still didn't help Olga's racing heart.

Without thinking, she let go of the railing support and raced to Sten's arms, clinging to him like a scared child. Sten wrapped his arms around her and stroked her hair. He looked at her and saw her eyes were shut tight. It pained him to see her like that.

"It's alright. You are safe. We are almost there, just a few steps more," Sten offered, raising her chin with a gentle finger. "Just keep your eyes on me, do not look at the river," he said.

Slowly Olga opened her eyes, nodding her agreement. She kept her eyes on him. The sun's rays poked between the trees, soaking her in a golden light; she looked angelic. Sten couldn't help himself; he stroked her cheek and offered a consoling smile.

"I must confess I am afraid, I....I.... can't swim," Olga admitted.

Reaching the other side of the riverbank safely, Sten stared at her bemused. She was a Viking. Vikings live and breathe the sea; they are born with sea legs to prepare them for voyages across much angrier water than this little river.

"A Viking who can't swim?" Sten whispered.

Olga was still locked in Sten's embrace. Since they reached the bank, she found she hadn't let him go either. She suspected he hadn't meant to let his thoughts slip from his tongue, but she heard them all the same. She had allowed herself to be vulnerable, opened herself up to one of her biggest shames, and he mocked her. Then, flushing pushed him away.

"What business is it of yours if I cannot swim? The ocean is far different from a rushing river like that," Olga snapped, jabbing an angry finger towards the running waters.

"I agree; the ocean is a far cry different. I just thought if someone were going to be afraid of water, the ocean would be far more of a concern," Sten shrugged.

Olga scoffed, rolling her eyes before storming away from

him. Sten looked back to the horses waiting across the river, instead turning to run after Olga.

"I meant no offence, Olga. I, too, have fears. It is normal," Sten yelled.

"Leave me be," Olga snapped.

"It is true. I hate snakes with a passion; they are nasty buggers. I am afraid of heights, and I fear everyone will forever think of me as a monster like Ulster. I am nothing like him; I wish others would see that too," Sten confessed.

Olga stopped, thinking about his thoughts. Then, turning back, she strode right to him, glaring into his eyes, searching his soul for the truth.

"You speak the truth. You would trust me with this?" she asked.

"You trusted me with your fear; it is only fair I trust you with mine," Sten answered.

He was being honest. It felt so good to finally speak his concerns to another human being rather than the small walls of his hut or ship's cabin.

Olga looked back at him. Sten couldn't place the expression on her face. She didn't look afraid or angry. Instead, she appeared to be questioning him.

"Wait here. I shall retrieve the horses."

CHAPTER 6

THEY RODE a bit further in silence. The sun was high in the sky, soaking them in a heat that made their wool clothes uncomfortable. Olga wiggled in her saddle, noticing Sten trying to hide his smile. Normally, she would snap and show him what it meant to laugh at her, but she smiled inwardly; she could imagine how strange she must look. Her stomach growled. She hadn't eaten since before dawn.

"Perhaps we should stop for a moment in the shade. My stomach aches. I need to eat. You must be hungry yourself," Olga suggested.

"I couldn't agree more," Sten replied.

Olga left Sten to start the fire while she snuck into the woods with her dagger drawn. The forest animals hid well. She could hear the rustling in the undergrowth and the branches of the trees above. She followed tracks on the floor to a small bush at the bottom of a mighty oak tree. A rabbit burrow sat below. Setting herself back, hiding in the trees, she tossed a rock at the bush, bracing herself for the rabbits' escape.

Three small rabbits, two brown and one white, raced for freedom, but they were no match for Olga's blades. Olga watched their path, how they zigged this way and that, finally tossing her knives through the air, instantly killing her prey.

"Your loss will not be in vain, my friend," she whispered to the rabbits as she carried them back to camp.

Together they sat skinning their lunch. Sten was much more skilled at it than Olga had anticipated; with two large slits and a sharp pull, he tore the fur off in one. Olga was impressed. Every move Sten made was paused as if he was silently asking her permission to help. It gave her much food for thought.

His confession about his brother answered her earlier questions. He went out of his way to be helpful and kind to show people he was not the same man, even if he made his moves without others seeing. She then realised why he had volunteered. He needed to prove himself. Lost in her thoughts for some time, Olga finally decided to speak.

"You are right. I am afraid. Not just of rushing waters that I cannot fight, but of....many things," Olga spoke softly.

"Such as?" Sten asked, spinning the rabbits roasting over the fire.

"Failing my mother. She relies on me.....being alone, not finding a family of my own. Being in the King's service can take you away from such things," Olga fidgeted with a stray thread on the hem of her skirt.

"Family is important to you, isn't it? I couldn't help but notice you seemed angrier that I left my brother alone than you are of me being guilty of similar crimes," Sten said, poking at the flames.

"Family is important to me. Lars and the others do not even know the reasons why," she gazed at the fire.

"Care to share?" Sten asked, finally bringing his eyes to meet hers.

Olga hesitated, but she could feel a pull towards Sten. She couldn't explain it. She had his undivided attention. She didn't know why, but she knew she could trust him with her secret.

"Years ago, my mother ventured to these shores. An Englishman forced himself on her. She locked herself away, afraid of her own shadow. I took it upon myself to be her carer.

Months later, she found she was with child. I didn't understand it then; I was so young. Once the child was born, my mother took one look and knew her time on these shores was done."

Olga felt freed, finally talking about her past. The tragedy may have been her mother's, but Olga felt it was her burden, too, seeing her mother suffer. All they had was each other.

"I do not know where she left my brother. All I know is she woke me at dawn, and we sailed back to Denmark."

Sten was lost for words. Instead, he offered a caring hand. Placing his hand on hers, he gave a sympathetic smile. Resting her hand on his, Olga smiled back. She still had another confession to make. And now she felt they were so deep into this that Sten needed to hear.

"I have heard rumours. About a giant, more Viking than English," Olga began.

"I have heard such rumours. Ulster rambled about his time with the British before he left. He wouldn't say what happened to him, just muttered madly. I heard one such rambling. A man who appeared Viking working with the British commanders, in a position of high command himself," Sten remembered.

"I believe he is my half-brother. I never knew what happened to him, mother still refuses to talk about him. He might not have been conceived in the act of love, but he did not commit his father's crimes…Just like you did not commit the ones of your brother," she added.

Sten sat up a little straighter, nodding his approval. Olga was sure she saw tears brimming his eyes. Someone finally saw him for who he was, a victim himself of his brother's misdeeds.

"Thank you, Olga," Sten whispered, giving her hand a gentle squeeze.

"Even when we returned to Denmark, mother was never the same. She never lay with another man. I was an only child with a mother in the shadows. It was…." Olga couldn't bring herself to finish, so Sten finished for her.

"Lonely?"

Olga nodded.

"I have to know if he is my brother. I do not even know his name. But to see his face, I know in my soul I will know. I would ride with djǫfull himself to find out," Olga admitted.

Her last words had not meant to slip from her thoughts, but they made Sten roar with laughter. Of course, seeing him laugh made Olga share a laugh too.

"That would be my brother. But, sorry, Olga, he is not here. So, you have been stuck with me instead," Sten laughed, turning his attention back to the rabbits roasting over the fire.

"A matter I am most grateful for," Olga said.

She didn't know why she had spoken the words, but she knew they rang true. Sten was nothing like Ulster, and Olga had regretted being so mean to him at the start of their trip. Her heart raced; she held her breath, waiting to see if Sten had heard her confession.

Slowly he turned to her, giving her the same questioning look she had given him at the bridge. Sten moved closer, watching to see if she was repulsed by him. But, instead, she sat still, her mouth open just a touch as her heart threatened to jump out of her throat.

He leaned closer. Close enough for their lips not to touch, but his breath could be felt on hers. Sten's eyes drifted from her lips to her eyes and back again. Olga didn't want to wait; she leaned in and closed the gap between them, letting her tongue slip past his lips.

Sten pulled Olga onto his lap, running his fingers through her hair. He felt himself grow, having her straddling him, so close yet so far.

CHAPTER 7

OLGA FELT her pale skin flush pink. She had not expected to enjoy kissing him, and she had liked it a lot. But panicked, she suggested they finish their food and continue on. The rabbit was a welcome distraction from her wayward thoughts. Olga watched out of her eye as Sten tore at his food, licking the charred remains from his fingers, before dunking a slab of bread from his pouch in the small stew they had made.

Sten grinned, catching Olga watching him. Several passing looks were shared, and Olga felt herself come alive. But they had a mission, and she only had a small speck of time to complete her own. She couldn't afford to waste a second, even if it was on a god-like Norseman.

"I think we should carry on with our journey once we have eaten. We can't afford to lose any more time," Olga said, taking another bite of the tough, dry meat.

"It will be dark soon; we can carry on in the morning," Sten said with a mouthful of food.

"We must find out what the British are doing with my brother. You said Ulster thought he was in a position of power? Is he working with them? Is he a prisoner forced to work against his people out of fear? Or something worse?" Olga said frantically, angry that Sten wanted to stop for the night.

"With respect Olga, until you lay eyes on him, you will not know if he is your brother," Sten said cautiously.

"I know he is. What other explanation exists for a man who appears as a Viking working for our enemy?" Olga snapped, tossing the remainder of her stew into the bushes.

Sten rapidly finished his food as Olga stamped out the remains of the fire and prepared to pack up the horses.

"Olga, I know how much you want that to be true. But I have a mission too. I must prove myself to our peoples before I become an outcast. We have to think about the community over ourselves. While I enjoyed our entanglement very much, I am not about to be sidetracked either. Perhaps you are right; we should keep moving. We have seen no sign of the British thus far. We need to make tracks before dark," Sten sighed, emptying the pot of stew and shoving it in his saddle bag.

Olga stared mindlessly at Sten. She watched as he mounted his horse and pressed forward. His words still rang in her ears. He had enjoyed their entanglement. But did he enjoy it as much as she? The feeling of her lips? She shook the thought off, jumping on her horse and following.

"Sten, wait," Olga shouted.

Sten pulled his horse to a halt. Waiting to hear what she had to say.

"I have an idea. A way we can both get what we want and complete our mission."

"Name it," Sten nodded.

"We make a pact. Five days. We find the truth, or we die trying," Olga suggested.

Sten hesitated, staring at her through a sideways glance. What was she saying?

"You have lost your mind, Olga," Sten laughed.

"My mind has never been clearer. I shall leave you to spy on the British; you can take all the glory for the discovery. I shall even help by telling you anything I find. I just need five days to find my brother. Please, Sten. He is all I have left," Olga pleaded.

Sten stared at her a second longer. What was he agreeing to? Then, shaking his head and rolling his eyes, he nodded.

"Fine. Five days, if you have found nothing by then, we go back together."

CHAPTER 8

By THE END of the fourth day, Olga and Sten had travelled further south than they first intended. They have come up with a story that they were travelling merchants looking for a new place to do business. But unfortunately, every town and village they arrived at was a dead end. They had spoken with village officials, whores, farmers, and even a child or two. But, so far, all they had discovered was everything they already knew. The British were mounting their forces, wanting to drive the invaders off their land.

No one knew where the British camp was or anything about a Viking working with them. Sten and Olga were beginning to lose hope. As the night drew near, it brought a strong wind and rainstorm, forcing the pair to take shelter in an inn.

The inn was quiet. The wind and rain forced everyone to stay home. Only a few passing travellers and locals drank inside at the bar. Huddled together in the corner by the fireplace, warming the chill in their bones, Olga and Sten finally sat down to voice their worries.

"Four days. For four days we have been travelling and so far nothing. Someone has to know something. What are we doing wrong?" Olga whispered, keen not to be overheard.

"Perhaps everyone fears that the British may find out they talked," Sten pondered.

"Did you see fear or apprehension in any faces? We were careful with our questioning. How much further shall we go?" Olga asked.

Sten thought it over for a while. Then, pulling a map from his pocket, he laid it on the table. It showed the distance they had travelled so far. To the west was the coast, venturing towards the isles on the other side of the British shores; to the east, more fields, villages, and mountain land. If they carried on south, they risked running right into the British forces head-on. This was supposed to be a mission of discretion; they couldn't risk being discovered.

"I don't see how the British could have travelled these parts with no one seeing them. Not a force like when they attacked," Sten worried.

"My point exactly. We can't go too far and risk getting side-tracked and not making it back in time to warn the others. What do you suggest?" Olga asked, taking a sip of her ale.

"The one place the British haven't attacked yet is by sea, correct? What if they travel from the capital to the west and use the mountains as cover? Cutting through the hillsides away from the villages? It's the perfect way to avoid being seen by anyone who may break words with your enemy. It is what I would do," Sten answered.

"Sten, you are brilliant. So tomorrow, we travel west towards the sea. That might take us another three days to get there. Is it worth the risk?"

"It's our last chance. We can't go back empty-handed," he concluded.

They continued to talk in hushed tones, developing their plan further. Day five would be spent travelling together. If nothing was discovered, Sten would continue to travel west, and Olga would head back home and try and catch the British on their way back before another attack. It wasn't a perfect plan by far. It was dangerous to split up, but they couldn't see any other way.

"You two need a bed for the night? We are closing soon, so finish up and decide," croaked the old, grey-haired barmaid who had wandered over.

"A room would be wonderful, thank you. We have been travelling so far, and I grow to try to carry on the eve. Plus with the wind...." Olga began, trying her best to act the part of a wary Scottish traveller.

"Ye, ye, close your trap. I'll get you a key," the Barmaid complained.

"You play the damsel quite well," Sten teased.

"Don't get used to it. I can't wait to rid myself of these rags and put on my armour," Olga grinned.

The barmaid returned with a single key. She tossed it on the table between them and stood with her hands on her hips. Her face was stern for a while before it broke into a happy cheery smile. The sudden change was unsettling to both Sten and Olga.

"Ah! The bloom of young love. How I miss it. That's how it was with Colin and I. He was a fine specimen, but he perished on a winter journey some three years past. Anyhow, your room is at the top of the stairs, the second door on the right. Enjoy your stay," she smiled before wandering off to converse with the other patrons.

"Young love?" Olga asked, blushing as she did.

"She thinks we are husband and wife, perhaps travelling after our wedding," Sten said, trying his best not to laugh.

"Would being married to me be so terrible? How you wound me so, my dear Sten," Olga mocked, pretending to cry as she fanned her face.

Sten burst out laughing, and soon after, Olga joined in. It was the only thing they could do to ignore the awkward tension growing between them. Two people, not lovers, sharing a bed?

"I shall take the floor. Come, we better get some rest. We leave at dawn," Sten stood, offering Olga his hand. Then, tossing a few silver coins on the table and waving at the barmaid, they ventured upstairs.

The room was tiny, barely big enough to house the small bed in the centre. There was no room for a man, even a slightly shorter Norseman like Sten, to sleep on the floor.

"Well....this is....intimate," Olga chuckled.

They shared a look as Sten removed his cloak. They hadn't been so close since that afternoon in the woods. Olga felt her face grow pink as she remembered their kiss. From the tension in Sten's jaw, he, too, remembered. It was a wonderful kiss. How could either forget?

Sten walked across the room and settled into the small uncomfortable wooden chair in the corner. It creaked and complained against his weight. He barely fit on it; it looked like it was made for a child.

"Come now, Sten. Do not be so bashful. We are adults; we are warriors. Surely, we can share a bed for one night," Olga said, slipping off her heavy skirts and sliding under the itchy wool blanket in nothing but her small cotton slip.

"I,...um...." Sten stuttered, his mouth suddenly dry.

"This bed is big enough for the both of us. I do not know about you, but I travel better on a good night's rest," Olga said, turning away to face the window.

Eventually, Olga heard the thump of Sten's boots, his belt dropping to the floor, and felt the bed shift as he crawled in the other side. The bed may have been big enough for the two of them, but the blanket barely covered one. The wooden shutters covering the windows were broken from the constant battering of the elements. Rain rushed outside, and the wind forced a chill through the room.

Olga tried to hide her shivers, but being so close, Sten would have to be an imbecile not to notice.

"Come closer; we can share body heat to keep warm," Sten offered.

"Um...." It was Olga's turn to be speechless.

"The blanket will not cover us both, and you said it yourself. It's just one night."

Slowly Olga moved closer, pressing her back against Sten's chest. Then, with his thick wide arms, Sten wrapped the blanket over them both, pulling Olga closer, stoking her bare shoulders in an attempt to warm her chill.

"You are freezing," Sten whispered.

His breath on her neck sent a new chill up her spine, the hairs on the back of her neck stood on end, and she released an involuntary gasp. Her body reacted as her back arched, and her hips rocked. Sten grew still. His hands stopped, but Olga could feel his heart pounding against his chest.

Olga rested her head against his collarbone; reaching around, she stroked his thighs.

"You are cold too. Perhaps I should return the favour to keep you warm," Olga said, her words breathy.

Rolling over to face him, she let her hands roam over the cold skin of his chest. Gentle flickers of the candlelight illuminated him in shadow. She was glad for the lack of light, for he might see her ogling his masculinity. Much to Olga's surprise, he had left his pants on, probably out of respect for her, but right then, it was much to her annoyance.

Olga could feel Sten quivering under her touch. He fought against himself but longed for her touch. Olga took his hand and placed it on her thigh. Slowly, their hands began to explore each other. Veiled as an attempt to keep each other warm, they fooled only themselves. Sten's hands roamed over Olga's chest, pawing at the cotton barrier between their skin. Olga ran her fingers through the small thicket of hair across his chest. It travelled down his torso to the hidden part below his waist.

Olga may have been afraid of water, but she had never been afraid of going after what she wanted. And in that room, she wanted Sten. Keeping her eyes locked on his, she leant closer, letting her lips linger a touch away as her hand slid under his trousers. She made her descent tantalisingly slow, while basking in Sten's gasps as she wrapped her fingers around the hard girth of his cock.

Slowly, she stroked his length, paying close attention to gliding her thumb over the head. Sten closed his eyes, and his breathing intensified. Teasingly Olga flicked out her tongue, licking his lips as she stroked harder, faster, until Sten moaned deep in his throat. As Sten's pleasure grew, his eyes widened. His lips crashed down on Olga's. His tongue danced with hers as his hand lifted her slip and his fingers traced up her thigh.

As Olga continued to stroke him, Sten pushed his fingers inside Olga's tight, wet opening. Following her lead, Sten stroked the aching bud between her legs with his thumb until she bit her lip to stop herself from crying out his name.

Olga rocked her hips against Sten's hand, her hand working magic on his cock. Their lips met once again. It was wonderful – A distraction from their worries of war, fears, and failures. It was too distracting.

Suddenly, the door to their room bust open, and four British shoulders stood at the helm. Olga and Sten had been found by the very thing they sought. Unfortunately, they hadn't been as discreet with their questioning as they believed.

"Grab them!" ordered the tallest man as the other three rushed the room.

CHAPTER 9

UNARMED AGAINST FOUR heavily armed soldiers, Sten and Olga didn't stand a chance. Outside the inn stood a large wooden horse-drawn cage made of solid iron bars. Four horses stood ready to drag Olga and Sten to their fate. Shoved inside, their clothes were tossed in with them. The soldiers laughed at catching them in the act – literally.

A few villagers had heard the commotion, standing outside their homes watching as the cage pulled away, heading south out of the village. Captured by the British, Olga and Sten only had each other. The few weapons they had were tucked in their saddlebags and seized. Olga still had one dagger strapped to her thigh. But one dagger against four men? She didn't like those odds.

"How are we going to get out of this?" Sten asked as the cage rocked from side to side on the muddy jagged road.

"Get out? Can't you see we have an opportunity here," Olga practically cheered.

"Opportunity? Have you lost your senses?" Sten argued.

"Quiet back there!" yelled one of the soldiers directing the cart, shoving a stick through the bars sharp into Sten's side.

"Olga, we are unarmed and outnumbered. We do not stand a chance if they take us to their camp. Our best bet for survival is to escape. If we can get them to stop the carriage….," But Olga didn't want to hear it.

"Sten, I'm not going home. We had a pact. Five days. I still need to find my brother. I am so close I may never get another chance," Olga whispered.

Sten was torn. He knew how much finding her brother meant to her. He hadn't intended it to happen, but he had fallen deeply for her. Ever since the moment she clung to him on the bridge, he could still smell the berries in her hair. She had opened up to him, and he had shared his fears with her. He had never felt comfortable doing that with anyone, yet she made it easy. Olga was a proud, determined, and strong woman, traits he found he greatly admired. If he were honest with himself, he would follow her anywhere. But Sten was no fool; he could see no sense in willingly going unarmed into enemy territory.

"Olga, I want to help you find your brother, but…."

"But nothing, Sten. You say you want to help me, then help me," Olga insisted.

"Olga, see reason here. How can you find your brother if you are dead? Do you think these men will listen to us? Ulster escaped by sheer dumb luck and his sneaky, cruel ways. We may not be so lucky. Our best chance is to attack when they open the cage, escape, and come back with greater numbers."

"Sten, it took us almost five days to get this far. I can't go back now," Olga cried.

Grabbing their clothes, which were now soaked from the rain, Olga and Sten continued to argue. Sten needed to make her see reason, but time had already run out. The British camp sat just through the woods on the hillside on the other side of the village. They had unknowingly rode straight into the enemy camp.

The carriage stopped suddenly. The horses neighed in protest at the tug on the reins. Swords were drawn, ready for an attack, and the cage door was pulled open. Sten was grabbed first, and a blade held to his throat. Two more troops ran in, grabbing Olga by her hair, trying to control her as she lashed out. She might be where she wanted to be, but she wouldn't stand being handled in such a way.

"Take them to the commander!" one of the guards ordered.

The British had taken over another small village claiming it as their camp. It was the perfect location. They were tucked away in the hillside, hidden by the woods and a five-day ride from the Norse settlement. The sound of the sea didn't escape Olga's ears; the sea was on the other side of the trees. Quickly, she worked out the village was far enough away not to be discovered but close enough to reach both the Point and the Norse settlement.

The pair were pushed and shoved through the village with soldiers spitting, cheering, and tossing things in their direction at their capture. Finally, the door to the inn was kicked open, and Olga and Sten were forcibly shoved inside.

Standing, waiting for their arrival stood the commander – A tall, slender man with a short dark beard and an angry face. He wore a simple white tunic emblazoned with a large red lion. Large brown leather gloves travelled up his arms. His chainmail under his clothes clinked as he walked. But, even inside, he proudly wore his simple metal helmet on his head.

"Well. Well. Well. What do we have here? Vermin spies? Did you think we were stupid enough to fall for your foolish disguise? We have been following you for days," the commander taunted, stepping closer and examining them from head to toe.

"I hear you have been asking questions. Well, I have a few of my own," the commander grinned as he stroked Olga's cheek.

Anger flashed through her; she growled in the back of her throat before spitting square in his face. Instantly, the commander struck Olga across the face with the back of his hand. Hitting her with such force, she fell to the ground. Sten attempted to break free, but the commander was too fast. Pulling a blade from his belt, he held it to Sten's throat.

"I wouldn't if I were you," he snarled. "Pick her up!" he ordered as he wiped his face clean.

Olga roared as a soldier grabbed her hair, pulling her to her feet. Then, swiftly spinning, she brought her knee to his groin, pulled her dagger, and prepared to fight. Then she saw the commander with a blade to Sten's throat, a tiny sliver of blood already drawn.

"One more move and I kill him! Understand?" the commander roared.

Olga dropped her blade and kicked it away. Then, glaring daggers at the commander, she clenched her jaw tightly shut. They would get no answers from her.

"What settlement are you from? Danish? Norse?" the commander asked, sitting down and leaving Olga and Sten to the mercy of his men.

Neither answered, keeping their faces blank and their lips tightly sealed.

"Don't play the fools; I know you speak my language," the commander taunted.

Still, the pair said nothing.

The commander found their defiance amusing. He continued with his questions. Where are they from? Who were they looking for? How many forces did they have? Did they know the British's location? Each of his questions was met with stony silence. Finally, the commander's face darkened, his brow furrowed, and he slammed his fist on the table.

"My patience grows thin!" his voice boomed.

Waving his hand, he gave an order. Sten received a punch to the jaw, while Olga received a slap to the cheek. Instinctively, they both reacted to the other being attacked but were caught before they could fight back.

"Interesting. Gentlemen, it appears we have two lovers in our midst. See the way she angers as we strike him. Look at the hatred in his eyes as your hands lay upon her," the Commander taunted, his men laughing with him.

"Take her! We will force the answers from her lips if we have to. Or would you prefer to watch?" the commander chuckled.

Evil dripped from his every word. This man was just like Ulster. A monster. Olga cried out as two men grabbed her and pulled her away. It was too much for Sten to handle. With a battle cry, Sten broke free from his captures, breaking a jaw, leg, and a couple of ribs of the soldiers who tried to stop him. Lunging towards Olga, Sten was immediately stopped.

A beast of a man filled the doorway behind him. Considering his size, he had moved so silently that neither Olga nor Sten had noticed his arrival. He had hair as golden as the sun, eyes as blue as a new day's sky, and angular features. All Olga could do was gasp and stare as the man slammed Sten to the ground.

Olga couldn't believe her eyes. It was like looking in the mirror. This man shared all her features, and her mother's eyes and hair. The Viking beast, the rumours spoke of, she had found him. Bringing her elbow up, she broke the nose of one of the troops holding her. Twisting, she grabbed a knife from his belt and stuck it in the ribs of her other captor.

She had dreamed of finding her brother for so long. Finally, she had almost given up hope. She had so many questions to ask, so much she wanted to say. She ran to him, but before she could utter a word, he grabbed her shoulders and tossed her against the wall.

Olga smashed into the wall, hard. Trinkets from a shelf fell to the floor with her. The air was stolen from her lungs, and lights flashed in her eyes. Her ear rang, and she lost all sense of the world around her as her back was taken over with pain that flowed through every inch of her body.

CHAPTER 10

OLGA GROANED ON THE FLOOR, struggling to stand as pain wracked her body. It was too much for Sten; he couldn't bear to see any woman hurt, especially the woman he realised he loved. Troops lunged at him, trying to stop him from retaliating. They were not strong enough to contain Sten, especially not now that his anger had erupted inside him. Sten slammed his head into the nose of the nearest troop. Sten punched and kicked his way free, tossing men over his shoulder like sacks of flour. Then, grabbing a fallen sword, Sten attacked; he wanted blood. Olga's rumoured brother or not, the beast of a man would bleed for hurting her.

"Stop him!" yelled the commander.

Sten made his way through the tidal wave of force trying to stop him, edging closer and closer to the man he wanted to hurt. Sten hadn't noticed Olga rise until she blocked a sword from cleaving off his head.

"I'll get the commander," Olga yelled over the noise kicking over a table to block the troops from advancing.

It was a free for all. And it quickly became apparent that no matter how talented Olga and Sten were as fighters, they would lose this fight and possibly their lives.

"Olga, we have to go!" Sten yelled.

Olga felt a blinding pain smash through her skull as a troop bashed her over the head with a chair. She fell to the ground and watched in horror as the man she suspected was her brother disarmed Sten. All time appeared to stand still as she saw Sten fall with blood gushing down his face from a nasty gash on his forehead.

The man held a sword and raised it high, intending to kill Sten. Olga felt her heart stop; she was too far away to jump and help. She did the only thing she could and prayed to the gods her plan would work.

"Brother! Stop!" she yelled.

He turned to her and his face blanked. His eyes grew wide, seeing exactly what she did, a mirror image of himself in her. He held his sword dangerously close to Sten but couldn't pull his eyes from Olga. Uncertainty lay thick in the air.

"Attack! We are under attack!" screamed a voice from outside.

The cry couldn't have come at a better time, giving them a moment's pause in battle. Sten kicked the sword out of the stranger's hand and swept his feet from under him.

"Vikings! Norsemen! They are everywhere. Call to arms!" cried the voices from outside.

Running across the room, Olga reached for the man she had been searching for her entire life – A man who could free her fears of loneliness and give her the family she had always craved. Sten. It was always Sten. Helping him to his feet, she made her way to the door.

The screams were true; the cavalry had arrived. Vikings from the Point charged in from the shore behind the trees, and combined forces from the Norse settlement charged in from the village yonder. When Olga and Sten had not arrived back with news, their people grew worried. It wasn't long before word broke out about a Viking force making its way through the countryside. From there, they tracked down the commotion in the British camp, knowing that Olga and Sten had to be in the thick of it.

The stranger stared, watching Olga leave. Then, finally, they locked eyes. And the realisation hit Olga like a brick wall. She had searched all her life for her long-lost brother and built an image of their reunion in her mind. But this man was not the brother she had prayed for. He would never be one of her people; he was a Brit. The enemy.

Outside, flaming arrows lit the night sky, and the cries of death echoed through the camp as the Vikings brought down all the power of Odin to protect their own. Olga wrapped Sten's arm around her shoulders, using her body weight to carry them both. He was hurt, and she needed to get him away before they were attacked.

"Wait!" yelled a thick British voice laced with curiosity.

Olga didn't stop. She needed to protect Sten the way he had tried to protect her. A large hand grabbed her shoulder, forcing her to stop.

"You called me brother," the man said.

"I did," Olga replied.

"Are you my sister?" he asked, confused.

"I believe I am," Olga nodded.

Olga stared back at her brother, waiting for him to react. But, instead, he stood examining her; pain filled his eyes, everything he had ever known shattered by a single word.

"We can't stand around here. We will be killed. Come with me," Olga pleaded, hoping against hope he would oblige.

The stranger's face hardened, and the moment of uncertainty was lost forever. He no longer looked at Olga with curiosity. He no longer looked at her as the mirror image of himself. Instead, all he saw was the enemy.

"We share a face, you and I, but your mother didn't leave you behind to die. So, I will grant you this one mercy. Run. Next time we meet, I will not be so kind," he said, turning and leaving her world to shatter around her.

Olga stood watching him leave. The world fell silent around

her. She had completed her mission. She had found the man she believed to be his brother, and he had rejected her.

"Olga, we must go," Sten insisted gently.

"I almost....you are right, come," Olga said, her mind now focused on her new mission – Making it out of the camp with Sten. Alive.

EPILOGUE

THE COMBINED force of the Point and the Norse had forced the British to flee their own camp. The commander had escaped, but that didn't matter. The British had received the message loud and clear. The Vikings were not to be messed with.

Back at the Point, Olga and Sten had reported their findings. And Olga had retreated from the group soon after. She had not been the same since that night. She felt like a failure. She had found her brother and lost him in the same night. All her life, she had dreamed of finding that lost connection, having blood close. Instead, he had seen her only as his enemy; he didn't know her heart. He had offered her favour letting her and Sten escape, but the threat was clear. He wouldn't hesitate to kill her if they met on the battlefield.

Sten found Olga standing by the shore, staring off towards home. She had done that every day since her return, hoping the waves would give her the answers, but no matter how much she waited, the answers didn't come.

Sten sat in Olga's hut waiting for her to arrive, deciding it best to give her the time she needed to grieve. Sten felt like he had waited all day before Olga finally returned, the setting sun basking her in a golden light as she opened the door.

"Sten," Olga said, surprised to see him.

"You have been absent a lot lately. I came to see if you are well."

"I am fine," Olga lied.

Sten walked over and took her face in his hands.

"Your mouth may say the words, but your eyes tell me you are lying," Sten spoke softly.

"What do you want me to say, Sten? We failed. I failed."

"How?" Sten asked.

"I found and lost my brother in the same breath. We didn't even do much good on our mission."

"We laid eyes on the commander and several officers. I'd say that was a good find."

"We had to be rescued, Sten. How is anyone to trust either of us again if we fail at such a simple mission? Even Ulster managed to escape them," Olga complained. "But, our people came to rescue us because they grew worried for both of us."

Sten looked back at her, not believing her words.

"They might have acted harshly at first, but our people care for you too," Olga smiled.

Sten pulled her close, wrapping her in his arms, never wanting to let her go. She had given him all he had ever wanted; acceptance for who he was, another soul to see him for his heart.

"I am sorry about your brother," Sten kissed her head.

Olga stayed silent, stewing on her thoughts. She had been too busy remembering his rejection to look at the situation as a whole.

"He had wavered. He could have killed us both, but he let us go. So, there may still stand a chance to change his mind," Olga grinned.

"That's the spirit," Sten offered.

"For now, I should set my mind to more important things," she continued.

"Such as?" Sten asked.

"We are together, safe. I have to admit I rather enjoyed our partnership. We make a good team," Olga blushed.

"The best," Sten grinned back.

Olga pulled him close, laying her lips on his for a moment before gently leading him deeper into her home.

"I can think of another partnership we could start," Olga winked.

Sten laughed but didn't stop her from leading the way.

"We got in trouble for that last time, remember?"

Olga's face grew serious, her eyes hazy with lust. "I live for trouble," she growled, shoving him back against the wall.

Olga tore off Sten's tunic baring his chest to her; she nipped at his chest, slowly sinking to her knees. Her eyes did not leave his as she teasingly freed him from his trousers, scraping her nails along his thighs. His thighs were a particular favourite of hers. They were strong, defined. And she remembered the night in the inn where she had made them tremble with just a simple touch.

Sten watched as she took him in her hand, teasing, stroking, opening her mouth, taking him in slowly. Sten sucked in a breath, gripping her hair as she rolled her tongue up and down his cock. Sten watched as she went to work; slowly, she took him deeper. He could feel himself at the back of her throat as she sucked him deeper. He loved watching her please him, the joy in her eyes as she made him weaker. Skilfully, Olga massaged him with her tongue. Reaching up, Olga stroked him as she went, making sure all of him got a piece of her; his knees began to tremble as his pleasure built deep within him.

Sten groaned, moaning her name as she worked him hard. Finally, he couldn't hold it much longer. She felt so good, and she was enjoying the act as much as he made it all the more pleasing. Finally unable to control the force brewing inside him, Sten spilt his seed, feeling like his legs might give in beneath him. Olga stood, keeping her eyes on him as she licked her lips and cleaned off the remnants of his ecstasy.

"By the gods woman….," Sten panted.

Without another word, Sten scooped Olga in his arms and

rushed her to the bed. Tearing at her clothes, he laid her down. He pulled her to the edge of the cot, spread her legs wide, and rested them on his shoulders. He wanted her to feel the maddening pleasure she had given him moments before.

Sten nibbled up Olga's inner thigh before his tongue slowly stroked her opening, tasting her pleasure at pleasing him. She tasted sweet like honey and wine; Sten needed more. Spreading her open wider, he tantalised her, flicking, sucking, and licking until Olga's knees shook. Olga reached for him, holding his head in place, not wanting his teasing to end.

Sten slid his fingers inside at the same time. Olga jerked against his mouth as sensations new to her took hold. Olga bucked her hips forward, wanting more, needing more. Olga moaned; her body felt like it was on fire as warmth spread from between her legs to her stomach. Sliding his free hand up her chest, Sten took her breast. He pinched and teased her nipples. Olga moaned louder, her nipples had craved his touch. He sent shivers down her spine. Every nerve in her body sang as he worked his mouth and fingers faster. Olga convulsed against him. A wave after wave of ecstasy shook her to her core.

"I need more Sten," Olga panted, a new hunger in her she had never once felt.

"Then take it," Sten growled.

Olga sank to the floor with him; straddling his hips, she climbed on top and slowly slid down his thick cock, eager to accept him. Olga began to grind her hips, rising up and sliding the entire length of him, feeling every inch. Sten massaged her breasts, flicking the tip of his tongue across her aching nipples. The sensation drove Olga wild; she bounced on him, feeling their pleasure growing as she pulsed around him. Finally, Olga cried out, her pleasure building new intensity as she rode harder, feeling every part of him.

Sten growled his pleasure in Olga's ear. A primal growl that spoke to her in a way that commanded her release. Taking her hair in his hands, arching her back, Sten sucked on her neck. It was all it took for Olga to scream out his name. Olga clenched herself around him as her juices soaked them both before she collapsed, gasping for air into Sten's waiting arms. As they lay panting, Sten thought this might be the start of something special.

THE END

Did you enjoy the Sten and Olga's story?

Please review it on Goodreads, or Bookbub.

BIRGEN

FELLED BY A SWORD MAIDEN

PROLOGUE

VELIKA WAS STRONG. She was the bravest Norse sword maiden of her clan and proud to a fault. For years she had been second in command to her friend Triska. With Triska off at the Danish settlement at the Point, it was Velika's time to lead. Velika's settlement was different from most, being women-led. But they had proven time and time again that they were built for success.

The women of Velika's settlement had done just fine without men thus far in crucial leadership positions. Triska had been selected by the Norse King himself to lead the first Norse settlement in the Isles. He had no objections when Triska appointed Velika as her second. The men didn't complain, knowing how the pair were born to lead. Both women were victorious warriors in their own right. However, their most important trait was that they cared. They cared about their people, their men and women, and they treated everyone equally.

Velika loved the balance of life in her settlement and certainly didn't need big brawny Danes interfering with the status quo. The main problem was several Danish longships were due to arrive at the settlement any day now. Even if it was agreed upon as part of the Danish and Norse's new alliance, that didn't stop Velika's growing feelings of unease. The settlement felt like it was being invaded again, and she would much rather handle things herself. As if the Danish arrival wasn't problem enough, it wouldn't be long before the Norse longships from the Old Country arrived…Upon hearing the news of the British attack, the King was sending reinforcements to the settlement. Velika wasn't looking forward to either arrival one bit.

Since Triska left with her Dane, Lars, Velika had thrown herself into rebuilding the settlement. The British had almost destroyed her home, but Velika wasn't giving up without a fight. She busied herself with work to keep her mind off her incoming guests. She was setting up huts for the women, children, and most vulnerable first, helping the healers with the wounded and reinforcing the outer walls and gates against any upcoming attacks.

"What?" Velika asked. She was too busy, lost in a world of her own, that she had missed the question.

"You seem distant since Triska left," Estrid said.

Estrid was one of Velika's toughest sword maidens and a trusted friend. Whenever Velika needed to blow off some steam or wanted to strengthen her skills with sword and shield, Estrid was the one she turned to.

"How so?" Velika asked.

"Well, you're busying yourself with tasks you don't need to. You are stressing when everyone knows you were born to lead. You complain about the Danes a lot," Estrid answered, helping Velika erect the final wall of a new hut.

"I suppose I'm just adjusting to the fact we have allied with the Danes," Velika shrugged.

"Perhaps you want a Dane for yourself," Estrid chuckled.

That caught Velika's attention. It was well-known that Velika was yet to show interest in taking a husband. Many had offered their hands, and many had tried to woo her, but all had failed. Velika had no time or need for men, especially not a Dane.

"Explain yourself," Velika snapped.

"Well, the Norsemen do not seem to grab your attention.

Perhaps a Dane is what you want instead," Estrid answered, choosing her words carefully as Velika glared her down.

"Not that it is any of your concern Estrid, but I do not want or need any man. Do I not help run this settlement perfectly fine without one?" Velika barked.

"Excuse me, Velika. I did not mean to offend," Estrid bowed her head.

"Know your place and to whom you speak or find your tongue forever silenced," Velika snarled, storming away from the woman she once considered a friend.

Velika barely tolerated the Norse men of her settlement, forever keen to keep them at a distance. That didn't bother them, though. They respected her and gave her the space she demanded. It had served her well thus far. Velika's mind raced with the fact that the settlement was about to be overrun. Norse and Danes travelled their way, and she barely had enough rebuilt to house the survivors of the last attack.

Velika stormed to the seafront; the waves always calmed her racing mind. Thoughts of ships arriving plagued her and her eyes were haunted too. Cresting the horizon were several long-ships coming from the east. As the vessels drew closer, Velika released the breath she had been holding. It wasn't the Norse ships; it was the Danes.

CHAPTER 1

A SMALL LONGSHIP docked at the shore near the settlement. Velika watched from a distance, close enough to keep the ship in view but far enough away where she might not be noticed. The boat was barely big enough to hold twelve men. Its sails are off-white and in a little state of disrepair, and the ship's prow was carved with a long decorative dragon head meant to intimidate. The sides were lined with battle-worn shields. Velika was not impressed. A small group disembarked, primarily men, but the odd woman was scattered in the mix. Velika had seen enough.

Anger brewed in her stomach. Even if she were not looking forward to her own people's arrival, she would prefer them to have arrived ahead of the Danes. With several other ships gaining speed, she was starting to feel outnumbered, out-armed, and claustrophobic. She needed to occupy her mind and busy her hands, lest she bury her axe in a Danish skull. So, she began to work.

Triska's hut, which was Velika's for the time being, had half burnt down. To her relief, it was in a state of easy-enough repair. She had spent much time over the days since Triska departed working on the hut, but not as much as she would have liked. She wanted her people to have roves over their heads before herself. The walls had been rebuilt, but the roof was the main issue, which was next on her list before she could happily move in.

Velika was busy digging holes to implant the roof's wooden support beams when she saw the Danes approach. She kept herself looking busy. Still, with one eye watching their every move, she stared as they scattered amongst the settlement. Anger raced in her blood as one approached her direction.

He was a tall man but still shorter than most of the men she had grown up around. He had broad shoulders, bulking arms, and a stride that beamed with pride. His hair was cut short, as was his blonde beard. He took pride in his appearance, and Velika couldn't help but notice how he seemed dressed a little more decoratively than the other Danes she had seen.

Velika had been staring too long when the Viking looked in her direction. A pleasant, welcoming smile lighted his face. Not interested in his smile or words, Velika left her task and began chopping wood at the other side of the hut.

"Impressive," the man said as he appeared around the hut.

Velika didn't look up from her task, bringing her axe down and slicing a sizeable thick slab of wood in two.

"May I inquire as to the whereabouts of your clan's leader?" he asked.

"Leader?" Velika asked, pretending ignorance.

She had no interest or patience in dealing with the Danes that day.

"Yes. I am the leader of this crew; we come from the Scottish settlement to break words with your leader regarding our alliance. My name is Birgen. May I ask yours?" Birgen inquired.

He was polite enough and seemed sweet, almost soft for a Viking, but Velika didn't care.

"I know nothing of any alliance nor who now leads our clan. I am merely a shepherd. Take your questions elsewhere; I am busy," Velika said, slicing another chunk of wood.

"Very well," Birgen bowed his head and left, much to Velika's satisfaction.

After a day of hard work, Velika's stomach growled. Grabbing a bowl of stew and a roll of bread, she headed back to her hut, preferring to eat alone. She hadn't spoken with Estrid since that morning. With all the new men floating around camp, she wanted her space. Little did she know, she wasn't going to get her wish.

"Do you think it funny? Your childish act earlier today?" Birgen's voice rumbled as he entered her hut.

"Do I think what's funny?" Velika asked, dipping her bread into her stew, not raising her gaze to look at him.

"I spent most of the day looking for you. I was laughed at several times before one of your sword maidens took pity on me and told me I had already spoken with the leader – *you*. How do you think that looks? We are forming an alliance against a much bigger enemy, yet you pass me off and make me look the fool," Birgen snapped.

Velika couldn't help herself, and she let out a small chuckle, then continued eating.

"What sort of leader are you? Do you even care?" Birgen barked.

"Do not think to question my leadership, *Dane!*" Velika snarled.

She had suddenly lost her appetite. Standing, she took her bowl of food outside. She fed it to the few goats that remained— ignoring Birgen as he followed her around like a lost pup.

"Your settlement is not the only one to suffer. People and structures have been lost on both sides. This is why we need to stick together. We formed this alliance to protect each other from a much worse enemy. Or are you too blind to see that?"

"Are you finished?" Velika asked, stopping in her tracks and finally facing him.

She grew tired of trying to avoid him and would much rather he get his words out and leave her be.

"You are nothing like Triska! Why she would leave an uncaring, cold soul like you in charge is beyond me," Birgen barked.

"You do not know Triska. And you certainly do not know me. If you do not like it here, you are free to leave," Velika challenged.

"Believe me, I would much sooner be protecting my home, *my* people than be here. For all I care, you and your people can jump in the sea and let Njǫrd the sea god deal with you all. However, I am a man of my word and know that more important things must be done. I can put my pride and my feelings for your kind aside. Can you?"

Velika said nothing.

"I am here under orders from Lars to co-ordinate our combined forces. I am here to work with you, not against you, but you are testing my patience. Many have been lost and injured after the last battle. I saw your bodies myself. Unless we work together, no one will survive the next wave of attacks!" Birgen growled, growing angry with Velika's attempts to ignore him.

CHAPTER 2

To Velika's surprise, she felt a little shamefaced about how she treated Birgen. Her intention had not been to treat the matter lightly; She knew the importance of the alliance. After all, she had pushed Triska on the point before it had been agreed upon.

"My apologies," Velika sighed. "My intention was not to leave you thinking I did not take this matter seriously. That said, I am unhappy with a foreign man riding into my settlement, thinking he can fix everything," she said.

"I do not think I can fix everything. I am here on orders," Birgen began, only for Velika to interrupt with a further point of her own.

"I am not some young maiden fresh into womanhood who needs protecting or rescuing. I am a warrior," Velika stood tall. "I had seen battles long before I began leading this clan. If you can't deal with a woman in charge, that is your problem, not mine," she firmly stated.

Birgen looked at her, confused.

"I do not take issue with a woman in charge. I take issue with being taken for a fool," Birgen replied.

"Then do not make it so easy. I agreed to this alliance, and I shall stick to it. That doesn't mean I have to like it. We await the arrival of more forces from Norway. Until then, this conversation is over. You are more than capable of finding a place to house and feed your men for the night. We can continue to discuss the coordination in the morning. For now, I have things I need to do," Velika insisted.

Velika continued to mend the roof of her hut, so focused on her work she hadn't noticed Birgen join until she practically bumped into him while turning the corner.

"What are you doing?" she grumbled.

"I am here to help in any way I can. We can discuss the alliance as we work. I talk better with my hands busy anyway," Birgen said, unclipping his furs and grabbing a large wooden beam.

CHAPTER 3

Birgen had been raised by a legendary sword maiden. He has never had an issue with women in positions of power and had nothing but respect for Velika. He may have been mad when she made him look the fool, but that was purely due to his wounded pride. If anything, it made him respect even her more. She showed him she wasn't one to be pushed around or bend to anyone else's will. He admired a woman with a mind of her own.

They might be on opposing sides, but Birgen was interested in discovering more about how she was a leader as he liked what he had seen so far. It also helped that she was a beauty. Long blonde hair that was almost white was tied high on her head and still travelled long down her back. Her almond eyes as blue as the sea could bore into a man's soul. She enjoyed living alone, without the help of men, and, as a result, had the strength of a man too. Birgen liked that she had more meat on her bones than most other women.

Reluctantly, Velika allowed Birgen and his men to help her fix the roof. Birgen grinned each time he caught Veika fighting with herself, clearly biting her tongue, trying to prevent another disagreement.

Birgen grew curious; she was strong, capable, and

commanded the respect of the men under her rule. Yet she was wary; it was plain to see. She avoided the men, especially Birgen. She was shielding herself, avoiding glances, and taking leave to eat alone. Birgen soon deduced that she was a woman who was hurting. Birgen wanted to know what had caused a woman such as her to be so closed off and scared.

It wouldn't be an easy task to figure it out. Whenever Birgen tried to converse, Velika offered only short, non-descriptive answers – Answers that would lead to the end of the conversation. She took her time answering the few questions he asked, choosing her words with great care. Birgen wanted her to see that he respected women more than she knew. But to do that, he would have to gain her trust.

"Velmka…"

"Velika," she corrected.

"My apologies. May I ask a question?" Birgen asked.

"Another one?" Velika raised an eyebrow, and Birgen was pleased to see an amused smile broaching her lips.

"Did you rebuild this hut yourself?"

"Mostly," she answered.

"You are skilled not only in battle and leadership but with wood. Your workmanship is impressive. You will have to teach me so I can help rebuild when I return home," Birgen offered.

"Flattery will get you nowhere with me," Velika snipped.

"It is not flattery if it is the truth."

They worked silently for a while before Birgen heard Velika's reply, her voice barely a whisper.

"Thank you," she said.

"How long have you been a leader?" Birgen continued.

"Triska and I have been here since our people first landed. It shall soon be our second winter here."

Slowly, Velika began to engage in more open conversation, telling Birgen all about how the King himself had granted Triska and her the duty. She told stories of their struggles with local villages when they first arrived but swiftly gained peace, and the settlement grew quickly. But whenever Birgen tried to ask things about her that were a little more personal, she would grow silent or snap. His favourite retort that she used was: *If you keep insisting on sticking your nose in business that is of no concern or importance to the alliance, I shall permanently remove it from your face.*

"I mean no harm but shall respect your wishes," Birgen conceded.

As the day grew on, Birgen found he needed to know who or what had hurt her so badly to make her lose trust in all men. He also found himself wanting to hurt whoever had harmed her. It broke his heart to see the subtle flinches she tried to hide, the way she would not meet his eye, and the way she would shy away. It pained him that she carried so much anger, using it as armour. He vowed to show her that not every man was to be feared or hated.

"I am glad war approaches," Birgen began being cautious with his words.

"How so?" Velika asked in surprise.

"If war did not approach, our people may never have got past our history. I think that is a shame. Your people are a credit to you and your leadership, and I am glad war brought us together, for what it is worth. I am a man who is always looking to learn, and I feel I can learn a lot from a leader and warrior such as yourself," Birgen said.

He made an effort not to use the word woman. She would see he respected her for her skills and mind, not her sex.

"Like how to mend a half-torched hut?" Velika joked, sparking joy in Birgen's heart.

"First of many lessons, I am sure," Birgen smiled back.

It was slow progress, but Birgen was happy to see they were starting to get along. She was still cautious around him, but she had softened. Birgen would never forget the first smile he saw on her face. A smile she had tried to hide, but he hadn't missed.

He also wouldn't forget the sweet chuckle she tried to hide at his poor attempts at cracking jokes.

The roof was almost fixed. It would need another day's work but would do for the evening. The sun was beginning to set, and others had started a fire preparing food in the centre of the camp. Birgen knew if he was to get Velika to trust him fully, he needed to give her the space she craved. He didn't want to push her before she was ready.

"Well, I do not know about you, but the smell of that hog is making me hungry. I am also tired. It has been a long day. It has been interesting meeting you, Velika, but I think it is time for me to take my leave for the evening," Birgen smiled, bowing his head softly.

"Oh? I suppose it is getting dark," Velika said, slightly disappointed.

"I fear I have been absent my men for too long today. I best check they haven't been causing mischief. Good night, Velika," Birgen smiled and headed off into camp.

CHAPTER 4

VELIKA CLIMBED down the ladder and watched as Birgen vanished between the huts and campsites. She wasn't sure what had just happened. Not only did she find Birgen easy to talk to, but she also found herself comfortable enough to venture opening up to him. He had made her laugh and been respectful. He was not what she expected from a Dane at all. Velika sucked in a breath as the thought hit her. She found herself liking the Dane.

Confused by her feelings, she checked over what little work was left in her hut. With Birgens' help, she had taken at least two days off what she thought she needed. Needing to distract herself, she tried to finish the rest before the sun finally set.

Keeping busy hadn't done anything to calm her thoughts. The settlement was alive with energy. The exchanging of stories, laughter, and even a flute or two encased the settlement in song. Velika decided that she had spent too long away from her people. She took a leisurely stroll through the camp, checking the wounded and getting updates on what progress had been made. She couldn't deny that things had progressed quite far with the Dane's and Birgen's help.

The Danes had brought a healer. The wounded were resting, their pains lessened, and some who were thought to be at death's door were now resting with loved ones by their side. The outer walls and the settlement gate were fully repaired, and there were talks of a possible expansion and more huts to accommodate. Velika might not like accepting the Dane's help, but she had to admit she was impressed. And grateful.

Heading back to her hut to settle in for the evening, she came upon Birgen with a few of his men around a campfire. It appeared they had set up camp by the gates to keep guard and to show the Norse they were not here to invade. Velika ducked around a tent to avoid being seen. Birgen appeared to be telling a story; his men laughed with him, patting each other's backs. Scanning the camp, Velika saw a few of her own men standing nearby; they too laughed along with Birgen's tale.

"What are you doing over there? Come join us," Birgen yelled, catching the men watching him.

Her men seemed wary at first until a sword maiden – Velika assumed she was Birgen's second – offered up a leather flask.

"We have ale," she chimed.

The camp erupted into cheers and laughter as the Norse settled in to join them. Velika was mesmerised; she couldn't pull her eyes away. Velika marvelled at how easy it was for Birgen to pull people together. She watched as their tribes' history and bad blood slowly melted into the night.

This alliance was well past overdue, she thought.

CHAPTER 5

CONSIDERING her conflicted feelings around the Dane the night before, she slept peacefully. Too peacefully. Sounds of hammering, orders being shouted, and the tell-tale sounds of an axe splitting wood woke her from her slumber. Then, swiftly dressing, she headed out. It was a beautiful sunny day, probably the hottest since she landed on these shores almost two winters ago.

The settlement was alive with energy, and everyone able had their hands full rebuilding. If they carried on at this pace, the settlement would be as good as new by week's end. Velika strolled through the settlement admiring the progress, beaming with pride at her people. That's when she saw it. Birgen had jumped straight back to work, as promised.

Birgen strolled over, offering Velika a good morning smile as he tossed the wood he had gathered on the floor. Velika looked away and continued her conversation with Estrid. Estrid gave updates, but even as Velika nodded along, the words did not reach her ears. Birgen's tunic clung to his chest, highlighting the wall of muscles underneath. His tunic left little to the imagination but was still tantalising enough to make someone wonder about the rest underneath.

Birgen pulled his tunic free, using it to wipe the sweat from his brow before tossing it aside and continuing to chop wood for the others. The sweat dripping down his chest highlighted a long, jagged scar running across his torso. Swinging his axe, he looked like a god. All the other women passing by stopped to ogle.

"He seems to have a string of admirers," Estrid grinned, nodding towards a gathering of women.

"Really? I didn't notice," Velika shrugged.

Velika didn't care about Birgen's display of rugged masculinity; she was beyond interested in men. Anything a man could do, she had made it her business to do it better, or at least to the same level. She had no need for a man. From her experience, men were egotistical, selfish, uncaring beasts. She considered them evil beings who needed to be avoided at all costs. So why had she been watching Birgen out the corner of her eye? Why had her pulse quickened and her throat run dry?

Without realising, her gaze drifted over. She couldn't pull her eyes away from him. She licked her dry lips, and her hands trembled as she admired Birgen's form and how his abs became taught as he raised his ae above his head. She watched how his shoulders bulged as he brought the axe down and how the sun reflected off his sweat, drawing her eye to the small thicket of hair running up his stomach and across his chest. Birgen had noticed her looking. He smiled and nodded as he picked up his tunic, wiping himself down.

Velika flushed; she hadn't meant to look. Right? Angry with herself for forgetting her past and why she had spent so long avoiding the company of men, she marched towards the well. How could she have let her guard down with him so soon? So easily? It had been so long since a man had her body reacting the way it was now. Her heart raced, her head spun, and her skin prickled. Gathering water from the well, she splashed her face, hoping her reaction was merely from the sun's heat and not from the rising heat between her legs. Resting her hands on the well, Velika steadied herself, searching her mind for answers that wouldn't seem to come.

"Beautiful day, is it not?" Birgen asked, joining her at the well.

Velika watched silently while Birgen took several sips of water before splashing his face.

"What are you doing here, Birgen?" Velika asked, her frustration evident in her voice.

"Hydrating," Birgen laughed.

"No, I mean *here*," Velika gestured around at the work he had helped with so far.

"I'm here to help," Birgen said, his confusion clear to see.

"You are here to help form a plan for the next attack. Yet we haven't done anything but discuss the impending war."

"And whose fault is that? I tried to reach out on my arrival," Birgen said, a slight grin across his lips.

Velika could see he wasn't trying to place blame or cause a dispute. He was amused.

"For that, I am sorry," Velika admitted.

"How about we discuss battle plans over dinner?" Birgen asked, stunning Velika even as her heart raced.

"I think that is best. I have been so transfixed on the immediate needs of my people that I feel I have neglected preparations for an attack. I suppose that is part of the reason I ignored you when you arrived. I worry sometimes I am not a good leader," Velika breathed, keeping her gaze on the water glistening in the well.

"Is this your first time leading alone?" Birgen asked.

Velika nodded.

"Triska would not have left you in charge if she didn't believe in you. You feel the need to question your leadership skills means you are already a good leader. I may have only been here a little over a day or two, but it is plain to see that you were born to lead. The settlement is alive with talks of how much the people respect you. Do not doubt yourself; I believe in you," Birgen said, catching his breath after another refreshing drink.

Velika's eyes shot up to meet his. She had not expected him

to be so kind. His words warmed her heart, and her lips crept up into a smile. Clamming up, Velika's mind raced. Why was she telling him this? It was none of his business, after all. How had he managed to get her to drop her guard? It was too much. Her heart pounded in her chest, but not the same way it had when he first walked over. This time it felt tight, a pressure that threatened to be suffocating. Panic.

"I shall see you at dinner then. Meet me in the council hut," Velika said, walking away without waiting for a reply.

CHAPTER 6

THE COUNCIL HUT was the biggest structure in the settlement. It was meant for gatherings and battle strategy meetings and big enough for half the settlement to enter, with a long table in the centre. Velika had spent longer than usual preparing for dinner. She had never been a woman overly concerned with her looks but found she grew frustrated when she couldn't braid her hair. Finally settling on simply trying it out of her face, she headed to the hut.

Birgen stood outside waiting, and he wasn't alone. With him stood several of his men, his second Olga, a sword maiden in her own right, and several of Velika's men. Her stomach sank. Had she expected him to arrive alone? She was the one who suggested the council hut; perhaps Birgen had assumed everyone would be involved. So why was she disappointed?

"Good evening, Velika. Shall we begin?" Birgen asked.

Velika glanced at the faces staring at her waiting for her command. She nodded and watched as everyone entered before her. She needed a few seconds alone outside to gather herself. She had grown comfortable around Birgen for unknown reasons, but the sight of all the other men unsettled her. Clenching her shaking hands, she held her head high and followed everyone inside.

Sure enough, dinner had progressed into a planning session. Wasn't that the intention? At the meal's start, Velika kept her eyes on her food, nodding along her responses and barely speaking a word. But, as the conversation moved on to sending out scouts, how to split the forces, and everyone fought to be heard, Velika grew increasingly overwhelmed.

"Enough!" Birgen's voice boomed, silencing the room. "We are giving the British what they want if we continue to argue with each other. All ideas will be heard and given thought, but we have to think clearly."

Velika soon found she couldn't keep her attention from Birgen; he commanded the room with ease. Her men responded to him in a way she didn't expect. He was a natural leader and an excellent strategist. His mind was incredible; he looked at every idea from every angle, analysing where the British could take advantage and how a plan could fail. He could combine the best parts of every plan to create something spectacular. The British didn't stand a chance. Quickly, Velika realised she not only admired Birgen in a way she had admired no man before, but she respected him too. A feeling that would typically unnerve her, gave her the power to speak her mind.

"While your plan is admirable, Birgen, I feel it would fair much better if we sent scouts up the coast, towards the Point and to the west. We can't afford to assume the British will attack from the south again. They know we have seen their skills twice and don't want to risk being predictable. If we cover the settlement from all angles, we eliminate the element of surprise. Once we have eyes on them, we can prepare an ambush. Why wait for them to attack what we have worked so hard to rebuild? Let us take the battle to them," Velika spoke up, amazed to see how many faces nodded and cheered along with her plan. Birgen watched in awe as she spoke.

"I agree. We do not want to sit in wait," he acknowledged. "We surround the settlement to protect it and split the forces. When we can set up an ambush, and once it is clear they are not attacking from the sea, we shall signal the rest of the forces to join us. Let us show the British how they underestimated the power of the Danes and the Norse. Together we stand, and together we shall win this war," Birgen cheered, and the rest of the hut cheered with him.

As the meal ended, Velika felt like a new woman. She was filled with pride in her people, self-confidence, and a new trust in the men she fought beside. She no longer questioned herself; Birgen was right. If Triska didn't trust her, she wouldn't have left her in charge. It was time she trusted herself too.

"I think that is enough for one evening. We'll wait for the rest of your people to arrive, inform them of the plan, and then we get to work. Cut off the beast's head before it bites back," Olga cheered, raising her cup in a toast.

Slowly, everyone said their good nights and left. But Velika noticed Birgen stayed behind. Velika was unsure what to say or do but grew happy that they were finally alone. It's how she thought the evening would be.

"You were wonderful this eve. You are so much stronger and wiser than you think. You should wear it like a medal of honour. Let the world know that Velika is a force to be reckoned with," Birgen grinned.

Velika didn't have a chance to process his words. She didn't have a second to respond. Birgen took hold of her hand and drew her close, stroking his thumb across her knuckles as her hands trembled. Birgen stroked her cheek, cupping her neck and kissing her forehead gently. Velika found she was shaking for a whole other reason than mere nerves. His gesture was sweet and caring and showed he was not a man to be feared or hated. On the contrary, he was a man she could trust.

When he looked down at her, she found she didn't want to pull away. She was lost in his eyes. Birgen lingered, his eyes darting across her face, wondering, gaging where her mind was at. Finally, he lowered his lips to her cheek before gently kissing her lips. His beard scratched her chin, but his lips were softer than she expected. Before she knew what was happening, she found she was kissing him back. A gentle kiss of intimacy, of two like minds connecting, healing.

"I shall bid you good night," Birgen whispered, placing one last kiss by her ear before leaving her alone.

Velika stood transfixed on the spot Birgen once stood. His kiss had been like nothing she had ever felt. It wasn't forceful. It was gentle, yet the power it held still radiated through her body. Her chest heaved as her breath came short and fast. All over, she was aroused for the first time in so long. She couldn't remember how long. She brought her fingers to her lips. Tracing the line of his kisses, Velika was left confused. What should she do now?

CHAPTER 7

BIRGEN TOSSED AND TURNED, finding that sleep would not come easy. He didn't know why he kissed her. It had felt right in the moment, and he didn't regret it. What stunned him was the fact she had kissed him back. He couldn't stop thinking about her. Birgen had been set on proving he was a man she could trust. She had still seemed wary when they first started dinner. But she came out of her shell as the meeting drew on. She shone, and the way she commanded her men was admirable. Thinking back on the day, he remembered how she couldn't keep her eyes off him when he chopped wood; how her gaze lingered on his chest, and how she had flushed when he caught her looking. Had she been harbouring feelings all along?

Birgen could still smell the sweet scent of Velika's hair, and the touch of her lips still tickled his own. If he hadn't left so abruptly, what else could have happened? Dare he dream of it? Dare he let his mind think of what her body looked like beneath her armour? What would it feel like to lay his hands on her skin?

Closing his eyes, his mind opened to the possibilities. She stood before him, slowly taking off her clothes piece by piece. Birgen's hand slipped under his blanket. Taking hold of his cock, he began stroking himself as he imaged Velika's naked body before him.

Birgen imagined what it would feel like to feel her large breasts in his hands, to hear her moan as he flicked his tongue over her nipples. He stoked himself faster, imagining his hand was hers, stroking the length of him. Birgen licked his lips, wondering what it would taste like to lay his mouth between her thighs. He groaned to himself as he imagined sliding himself inside her. He wondered how tight she would be, how it would feel to be covered in her juices.

His pleasure grew, making him grow harder as he imagined her beautiful lips around his cock. He ached to feel himself at the back of her throat, to feel her moan around him as she gaged on his length. His strokes grew ever faster as he pictured her plump backside smacking against him as he took her from behind. Finally, his pleasure grew to the point of no return when footsteps outside his door had him scrambling to hide where his thoughts had just been.

He ached as his pleasure faded. Whoever it was, they better have important news to feel the need to interrupt him during such an intimate act. Without knocking, Olga stormed inside. She had walked in on him doing much worse in the past, but there was no hiding from her. She could read him like a book.

"Did I interrupt? Would you like me to wait outside while you finish? Or should I go and see if one of your admirers can help you?" Olga teased.

"Calm your tongue, Olga. What do you want?" Birgen asked, running his hands over his face.

Olga looked uneasy. Something troubled her mind. She paced back and forth before taking a seat at the end of his bed, much to BIrgen's annoyance.

"I see the way you look at her, and I see the way she looks at you," Olga began.

"Jealous?" Birgen joked, but Olga's face stayed stern.

"Be careful with her, Birgen. She has been hurt," Olga warned. She knew the look of a woman who had suffered an unspeakable atrocity.

"What kind of monster do you take me for, Olga?" Birgen began. But Olga had a point to make, cutting him short.

"I do not doubt you, Birgen. But I have seen the look in her eyes, how she is wary of her own men and how she hides away. It is an expression I have seen in someone I care for. It's the undeniable look of a woman hiding her fear – A woman who has had a man force himself upon her," Olga finished, the pain in her eyes evident that the story was not her own but pained her all the same.

Birgen ran a hand over his face and sighed deeply.

"I thought that was the case. I just didn't want to believe anyone could do that to her. She hides it so well," Birgen nodded.

"She has had to," Olga said. "What are your intentions with her?"

Birgen shook his head. He felt guilty for longing for the way he did now that his worst fears were confirmed. His heart ached, and his anger raged at the idea of tears staining her face brought on by a monster of a man.

"I am not sure; I do not know I feel right now. Thank you for bringing this to my attention, Olga. Go and get some rest; I fear sleep will not come easy tonight. I shall walk the camp to ease my mind," Birgen said, waiting for Olga to leave before he dressed.

"I shall walk with you. I know you, Birgen. You will let your mind get the better of you. I shall meet you outside."

Birgen always felt better being closer to the sea. Something was freeing about the lapping waves and salt spray against his skin. Yet as he stood looking out across the shore, with Olga at his side, he found this time was different. The waves didn't ease his mind; they tortured it. The night was too quiet, yet the waves seemed angry. He had seen it before; the waves predicted what was yet to come. Evil approached.

"What plagues your mind, my friend?" Olga asked, seeing the tension on his brow.

"The waves, they are too angry for a night so calm. It's not a good sign. Evil is heading to these shores," Birgen answered.

"You are getting superstitious in your old age," Olga teased.

CHAPTER 8

BIRGEN REASSURED Olga that he would be alright and continued his walk alone. Letting his mind go blank, Birgen allowed his legs to carry him wherever they wanted. It wasn't long before he ended up standing outside Velika's hut on the other side of camp. He looked at her door, unsure of why he was there or what to do. Birgen turned to leave when Velika stepped outside.

"Why are you here?" Velika asked, pulling her blanket tighter around her to guard against the cold.

Birgen noticed how she didn't appear to have been sleeping either. She was still dressed from the battle meeting but minus her armour. He knew he had been almost silent, so he couldn't have woken her.

"I, erm.....sleep wouldn't come. So, I took a walk," Birgen stuttered awkwardly.

"And found yourself at my door?" Velika grinned.

"Sleep did not come easy for you either, I see."

"I'm not tired," Velika answered.

The conversation ran dry, but neither of them could pull themselves away. Birgen wanted to know what was going on in Velika's mind. Did she think of him the way he thought of her? Had she been kept awake wondering about him? And had she been able to stop thinking about their kiss?

"It is a beautiful evening, is it not?" Velika asked, finally breaking the silence.

"It is. Although the waves are angry," Birgen rambled.

"You ventured to the shore?"

"The water calms me," Birgen replied.

"Your mind needs calming? What troubles your mind? Let me help," Velika stepped closer.

A gentle breeze swept through the air, flicking stray strands of hair across Velika's face. Birgen instinctively brushed them aside, stroking her cheek as he did. Her lavender and rose scent filled his nose. With her too close, he felt himself straining beneath his clothes as his mind raced with the images of his desires.

Stepping back, he dropped his gaze. Olga's words circled in his mind. Birgen wanted Velika more than he had craved any woman, but he needed to take his time. He didn't want to scare or hurt her; he cared for her.

"I shall leave you to get some rest. Dawn will break shortly, and we have a long day ahead," Birgen bowed, turning to leave.

Shockwaves shot up his spine as Velika reached out to take his wrist.

"Wait, don't leave. Not yet," her voice was as soft as a whisper, but the power it held was enough to bring a man like Birgen to his knees.

Birgen's heart began to race. Velika didn't need to say anything. Her eyes spoke for her. Slowly, she took a step inside, bringing Birgen with her. Birgen followed, allowing her to take the lead. Velika stepped closer, closing the door behind them, her lips lingering near his neck. She was close enough to touch, but Birgen felt she was a mile away. He fought against every fibre of his being not to ravish her where she stood.

"Velika…."

"Shh," Velika hushed.

Velika reached up, tangling her finger in his hair, pulling him closer. She lay a gentle kiss on his lips. Their kiss was soft and tender but held the power of an intense passion. Birgen slowly trailed his hands up her sides, spinning her around and pinning her against the door.

"Are you sure?" Birgen asked as his hands trembled against her cheek.

Velika said nothing; she took his hand and tucked it under her skirt. She ran his hand up her thigh. Birgen kept his eyes locked as she pressed his hand against her opening, giving him permission for the pleasure they both craved.

His fingers stroked her, circling the sweet bud. Birgen watched as she rested her head back, her eyes closing, and she gasped at his touch. Birgen lay his head against hers, feeling her breathe against his lips as she moaned. His fingers spread her apart. Finally, he let his fingers push inside, feeling how tightly she clung to him. His fingers dripped with her juices.

Velika trembled under his touch as the pleasure spread from her thighs to her stomach, rising like a tidal wave. The sensation was an intensity with fire's power but the night breeze's gentleness. Her nails dug into his back, making Birgen strain harder; he longed to feel her around his cock. To feel her come apart with himself inside her. Finally, the pressure became too much, and Velika cried out his name as she came apart around him.

Her eyes grew hazy as she smiled back at him. Birgen pulled his hand to his lips, licking her juices from his fingers. Her eyes grew wild with lust and hunger. She tasted as sweet as honey, and he wanted more. Birgen scooped her into his arms and carried her across the hut to her cot. Setting her down gently, he lay her back.

Birgen could tell she was still a little reserved and didn't want to push her further than she was willing to go. But he wanted her to know how much her pleasure and happiness meant to him. So, pushing her legs apart, he rested against her, kissing her passionately. Their tongues danced before he made his way between her legs.

Velika gasped as Birgen sucked her bud between his lips. She arched her back as waves of ecstasy pulsed through her. Then, spreading her wider, Birgen let his tongue do everything he wanted. He entered her, stroked her, and lapped up her juices as she spiralled into ecstasy once more. But Birgen wasn't done.

Velika moaned louder, writhing under his touch. Her hands pulled at his hair as his fingers entered her, as his tongue played with her. Velika panted as pleasure ran through her, building and building inside her. Birgen waited until he knew she was about to come apart before sucking her between his teeth, sending her over the edge for the third time.

CHAPTER 9

VELIKA AND BIRGEN lay in each other's arms, kissing like love's first kiss. They were enjoying simply being with each other when a yell from outside startled them.

"An attack?" Velika asked.

Birgen listened as the yelling grew louder.

"No, something else," he answered.

They swiftly straightened themselves up, sharing one last love-filled smile before rushing out into the light of a new dawn. Crowds ran across camp towards the shoreline. That could only mean one with. A Norse ship had arrived.

"I guess reinforcements have finally showed up," Birgen said as they followed the crowd.

Velika was thankful for the distraction. She had no idea what came over her when she led Birgen into her hut. She didn't regret it, not in the least. But it was still a lot so soon. She admired how he had been gentle with her, letting her start things off, but then he took over, determined to give her a night's pleasure like she had never had before. She worried that if the Norse had not arrived when they had, she might not have been able to control herself with Birgen, which she still wasn't sure she was ready for.

Pushing through the crowd, Birgen and Velika stood ready to

welcome the new arrivals. They needed the extra forces. The Norse ship was bigger than any the Vikings had in their supply, big enough for at least twenty to thirty men. They had come with numbers, supplies, and new hope for winning the war.

Velika felt Birgen's hand entwine with hers as she smiled at her people. That is, until she saw it, a sight that sent her cold. Her pulse was racing, her eyes blurring, making bile rise in her throat. Ulster. The monster from her past. The monster she had tried so hard to escape from under his shadow.

"Velika?" Birgen asked, his voice laced with concern.

"It's....nothing," Velika lied, pulling her hand free.

She watched as Birgen followed her gaze until his eyes locked on the dark-haired man who was showered with praise upon arrival. He was tall and toned but not as powerful as Birgen or his men. A deep scar sat across his cheek, and one of his dark eyes was white. Blinded in battle, Birgen suspected. Though the man smiled at his people, Birgen could tell this man was the evil the sea had warned him about. Velika might not have told him, but her reaction was all the confirmation Birgen needed. This was the man who hurt Velika.

Without thinking, Birgen pulled his axe from his side, launching himself at the man. He swung his axe, but the man ducked out of the way. Birgen kicked him square in the stomach before bringing his fist up under his chin, knocking him to the floor. Men tried to pull Birgen back, but his rage only fueled his fire. Pushing them away, Birgen was on Ulster in a second with his axe to his throat.

Birgen didn't care that this could be seen as an act of aggression – A threat to the alliance. Dane vs. Norse on the Norse shores. Everything that they had worked for and needed to win the war lay on the edge of his axe's blade. But all Birgen could see was the monster who hurt the woman he was growing to love. That was something Birgen would burn the world for.

"Birgen stop! Let him up!" Velika roared.

"You would defend him? After what he has done?" Birgen yelled.

"This is not your fight. It is mine," Velika barked, grabbing Birgen's shoulder and yanking him back.

Birgen never let his eyes leave Ulster's face.

You can't take your eyes off a snake, lest it slips away, Birgen thought. The words his mother had been ingrained in him since as young as he could remember.

Ulster rose to his feet, laughing. He brushed off the sand and dirt from his clothes. His eyes darted to Velika, lingering with a sneer as he looked at her from head to toe. His vicious tongue wetted his lips before he turned his attention back to Birgen. Finally, Ulster appeared to have put the pieces together.

"Fiesty one, isn't she?" Ulster snarled, stepping closer to Velika.

"I wonder what new tricks you have learnt from your Dane. I can't wait to find out," Ulster snarled, laughing at his last words.

Birgen never got a second to react before Velika yelled out. Velika kicked Ulster square in the chest, forcing him back. Then, scanning the crowd who watched in shock and surprise, she grabbed Olga's broadsword from her hip and raised it to Ulster's throat.

"I have run from my home to escape you. I run no more. I am not the girl I once was, and I challenge you, *Ulster*, to Holm-gang!" Velika roared.

CHAPTER 10

HOLMGANG WAS a word that held a simple challenge yet spoke of unspeakable wrongs. Holmgang was not a simple duel. It was a fight that usually ended in death. The crowd around her gasped. For Velika to challenge one of her own, especially one who had just arrived with the intent to help, spoke volumes. The crowd formed a circle around Ulster and Velika, whooping and chanting their support.

Ulster grinned, thinking he had this fight in the bag, thinking that Velika was weak and scared. But he was wrong. Ulster pulled two small axe's from his belt, twisting them in his hand, waiting for Velika to attack. He didn't wait long before Velika cried out her battle cry and charged at him.

Years of anger, pain, hurt, and haunted memories fueled the raging fire inside her. She longed for revenge and felt a need to protect the women of her settlement. Ulster was no match for her; she had far too much at stake. He was a threat that needed to be dealt with. It would all end on these shores.

Birgen grinned at Ulster's look of surprise when he failed to land a single attack. Birgen's heart filled with pride when Velika disarmed him quickly and had Ulster running scared. Her attacks were fueled by anger but ruled by skill. Ulster attempted to claim another's sword, but Velika brought down her sword slicing his arm, blood drenching the sand. Velika swept Ulster's legs from under him. Grabbing one of his fallen blades, she buried it in his hand as he tried to defend himself as her sword met his throat.

Velika leant close to his ear, seeing the terror in his eyes, knowing he had been beaten.

"A trick I learnt from the Dane," Velika snarled.

"Velika, stop!" Birgen yelled, pushing his way onto the battlefield.

"Why? He deserves to die for his crimes," Velika sneered, pushing the blade deeper into Ulster's throat, tears threatening to leave her eyes.

"Dying from Holmgang is too honourable for him. Do not stain your hands with his blood," Birgen tried to reason.

Velika pushed the blade deeper causing Ulster to groan against the pressure and blood to trickle onto the sand.

"I do not intend to stain my hands; I intend to soak the earth," Velika yelled.

"If he dies during Holmgang, he will dine with his ancestors in the halls of Valhalla before the next British attack. Do not allow him such an honour," Birgen reasoned.

"You are right. Allow Odin to judge you for your crimes so he too can refuse you entry into Valhalla," Velika snarled.

Velika pulled Ulster to his feet, tossing him into Birgen's waiting grasp.

"Here standing before you is the monster known as Ulster," she informed the growing crowd. "A monster who preys on those he deems weak. Torturing women's bodies and minds for his own pleasure. A vile creature who will torture my mind *no more*! I would sooner see you fall to the British than look at you," Velika informed her people, spitting on the ground at Ulster's feet.

"Ulta!" yelled the crowd.

Outsider. Exile. Her people stood with her. Ulster was not

one of them. Suddenly, a scout galloped into camp, interrupting Ulster's impromptu trial.

"The British are here!" the scout yelled.

"Prepare for battle!" Velika and Birgen roared, rallying the troops.

Birgen shoved Ulster to the side, grinning at him as Ulster realised his fate. The Danes would not fight with him. The Norse would no longer claim him as their own. His fate lay in the hands of the British. His time was drawing to an end.

The settlement had more warriors than ever. Both Norsemen and Vikings fought side by side. They were a force to be reckoned with. Old blood forgotten, they shared a purpose in defeating the common enemy. Velika summoned her sword maidens. Birgen commanded his forces. With Ulster no longer holding the regard of his men, they bowed at Velika's feet, awaiting her command.

"How close are they?" Velika asked the scout.

"Approaching fast. But we have enough time to cut them off on the battlefield before they reach the settlement."

"Archers, man the walls, set your arrows a flame. Rain down all the power of the gods. Let's show these vermin what it means to go to war with the combined force of the Norse and the Danes!" Velika roared.

"If they want war! A war we shall give them!" Birgen hollered.

Cheers and war cries erupted as everyone readied themselves for the battle they knew was coming. Together, they rode out to surprise the British. Birgen did not worry that Velika could take care of herself but kept close by her side. It was his first time seeing her in battle, and he was mesmerised. She fought with the power of the Valkyrie.

Her attacks were precise, and her sword left no man standing. She moved with the elegance of a goddess, while her sword acted as a weapon from the gods. Confronting Ulster had freed her in a way she didn't know she needed to be freed. Birgen cut through his assailants while admiring Velika, falling madder and deeper in love with her with each drop of blood she spilt.

A cry for help called Velika's attention. Ulster was outnumbered, fleeing like the coward she knew him to be. The British knew the battle was lost. In an attempt to gain the upper hand, they made one last move. They wanted Ulster, thinking he would have information to help them win the war. Little did they know, he had only just arrived. He could give them nothing, but they would torture him all the same. Velika grabbed a bow from the cold dead hands of a British archer; pulling the bowstring tight, she let her arrow fly. The arrow embedded in Ulster's thigh brought him to his knees, giving the British enough time to grab him. Velika watched as he yelled for help. She felt nothing. She had the revenge she needed.

"That was cold," Birgen said, standing by her side.

"Casualty of war. Let them have him, he knows nothing of importance, and now I know the women of our alliance are safe."

The alliance was no match for the British. They outnumbered the enemy five to one. It was a short battle before the British called a retreat, but it was a battle doused in glory. History was written with British blood. Old enemies, now friends. Old rivals are now family. And two commanders shared a love they never expected.

The cheers of victory echoed through the land like a lullaby. Songs would be sung of this victory for generations. Velika and Birgen scanned the battlefield. They had taken a handful of painful losses, but they were still stronger in numbers than before. The land was littered with fallen enemies. They had won.

"I think this alliance might work after all," Velika grinned, grabbing a fist full of Birgen's tunic and pulling him to her.

"That sounds like you once doubted," Birgen grinned.

"I may have, but not anymore," Velika replied, pulling Birgen into a kiss of unrivalled passion.

EPILOGUE

A FEAST WAS PREPARED to celebrate their victory. The settlement was alive with new hope. People danced around the campfire, and couples shared an embrace. Drinks flowed freely that night; they knew they wouldn't have to worry. Birgen and Velika escaped back to Velika's hut. Wrapped in each other's arms, they continued the celebrations alone.

"We may have won this battle, but we can't keep sitting around waiting for another attack. We must do more, take the war to the British. Cut them off before they can grow their forces," Velika urged.

Her newfound confidence in her leadership made her mind free to think clearly. Velika's mind hadn't left the battlefield even as the celebrations roared around them.

"I agree, but not tonight. Allow us our victory," Birgen whispered, rubbing his nose against her cheek.

"If we know what they are planning, we can be more prepared," Velika insisted.

"I love this side of you. Your determination to protect your people. You are a woman to rival the gods, Velika," Birgen said, kissing her neck softly. "You want to make the first move in war. I like the way you think. It makes me wonder in what other areas you hold that thought."

It didn't take long for Velika to figure out what Birgen insinuated. Her own mind had been on a similar thing.

"I thought my views on that had been made clear," Velika teased.

"Maybe my mind needs a little refreshing," Birgen winked.

"Then let me make my intentions clear," she moved closer.

Velika pulled them both to their feet. Slowly, she began to remove Birgen's clothes. Releasing him from his tunic, she ran her hands over his chest, trailing kisses across him as her hands sank lower. Removing his belt, she released him, grinning to see he was already waiting for her. Stepping back, she pushed her tunic down her shoulders. With her eyes locked on his, she shimmied her dress past her hips and stepped out of it, laying herself bare in front of him.

Birgen stepped closer, letting his hands trail over every inch of her. His touch set her skin on fire. Velika pressed her hands to his chest, pushing him back onto the cot. Then, dropping to her knees in front of him, she ran kisses up his thighs, letting him know what she had planned.

Taking him in her hand, she stroked, watching him grow and loving the sounds of pleasure that escaped his lips. Then, taking him into her mouth, she began to lick him slowly. She rolled her tongue around him, teasing him. Birgen lay back moaning and hissing as she sucked and stroked him in turn. The more moans that escaped Birgen's lips, the more Velika sucked him hard until she had all of him in her mouth, touching the back of her throat.

It was almost too much to bear, but Birgen didn't want to lose his seed just yet. He had plans for Velika but loved how she took the lead. His ecstasy grew as she took her free hand and cupped his sack, massaging as she continued to stroke and suck.

"Velika….by the god's woman… I'm…." Birgen groaned.

That's when she stopped. Standing tall, she walked across her hut to the small table, leaning herself over and spreading her legs wide. Flicking her hair to one side, she looked back at him.

"I want you Birgen," she cooed.

Birgen leapt to his feet, striding across the room to her. Stroking her backside, he gripped her tight, spreading her further before gently pushing himself inside. Slow and tantalising strokes drove them both insane. He wanted to feel all of her, and he wanted her to feel all of him. He took his time until her moans grew loud and demanding.

"More Birgen, I need more," Velika moaned.

Birgen pulled her to him, arching her back and filling his hands with her breasts. Laying kisses on her neck, he buried himself inside her, pounding in quick short bursts until he felt he could go no more. Then, gently removing himself, he spun her around to face him, scooping her up and carrying her back over to the cot.

"I want to watch you as you come apart around me. I want to see that beautiful face in the throes of passion," Birgen growled.

Velika wrapped her legs around his waist and put her arms around his neck.

"Then take me, Birgen. Show me what it is to make love."

Birgen was all too happy to oblige. He wanted to worship every inch of her. He lay her down and kissed her from head to toe, taking his time with her breasts, relishing in her reaction. Slowly, he pushed back inside her, taking her. Velika moaned louder. Her fingers clawed at his back as her pleasure grew deep inside. Brighten made love to her until they both dripped, soaking in each other's sweat. Finally, Velika writhed as her pleasure wracked through her, taking over every part of her.

"Birgen, that was…."

"I'm not done yet, my love. I want to worship every part of you. To explore every part of you," Birgen said, kissing her with the passion of a thousand suns.

They made love until the sun was high in the sky the following day. Birgen worshipped her until her legs shook, and the entire settlement could hear her screaming his name.

THE END

Did you enjoy the Birgen and Velika's story?
Please review it on <u>Goodreads</u>, or <u>Bookbub.</u>

PIER

ALLIED WITH THE NORSE

PROLOGUE

PIER GREW tired of his leader, Lars, spending so much time at the Norse settlement. Alliance or not, the Point needed him. So, when no one else seemed to share Pier's concern, he travelled to the Norse settlement alone to bring Lars home. After almost a two-day ride, Pier arrived just as the rest of the forces returned from what looked like a heavy battle.

The wounded arrived on stretchers dragged by horses. The crowd had an air of victory, but the mood was sombre. The wounded were many. Heading the group rode Lars, Triska, and the two spies everyone had rushed out to save.

What happened? Pier thought as he watched from the edge of the gate.

Everyone who hadn't ventured out stood cheering at their arrival. Gravely wounded warriors were clinging to life. Angry fighters with superficial wounds perked up by the support from their brethren. They looked like they had been through a lot, yet they celebrated each other, returning side by side. Norse and Dane alike, acting like old friends.

Pier watched as Lars rode in, smiling like a love-sick puppy at the Norse woman known as Triska. She was a distraction; a distraction Pier didn't appreciate. Pier scanned the crowd.

People embraced; Norse and Dane shared tender kisses and helped each other. Alliance or not, Pier couldn't wrap his head around the display. How could they all so easily forget the bloodshed between their people? How could generations of history be erased in a second?

Pier folded his arms tight across his chest, shaking his head in disbelief and disapproval. He already had a list of things to discuss with Lars. The more he watched the interaction, the more issues he saw. Scanning and scowling at the scene that turned his stomach and boiled his blood, he noticed he wasn't the only one watching.

Suddenly, Pier found himself distracted, ignoring the warriors struggling to walk and ask for help. Instead, he went through the crowd to get a better look. His eyes rested on beautiful woman he hadn't seen since he'd arrived a few days ago.

She stood tall, wearing a simple dress and apron. She wore a cloak across her shoulders, the hood draped over soft brown hair. Her hair brushed across her face in waves before settling on her shoulders. She hadn't arrived with the warriors. Was she a farmer perhaps? Or a healer? Pier didn't know but wanted to find out. The closer he got, the more transfixed he became. She had skin as pale as the snow back home in Denmark but lips as red as the blood racing through his veins. Her eyes were small, angular, and almond-shaped with a hint of green like fallen autumn leaves. She was like nothing Pier had ever seen, and he longed to hear her name.

Stepping closer, Pier found himself trapped by a wagon carrying wailing, wounded soldiers in his path. Pier moved left and right, trying to make his way over to her, but fate continued to intervene. The beautiful woman turned to a friend by her side.

"How many wounded are there?" she asked.

At that moment, Pier felt bile rise and burn in his throat. Her accent told him everything he needed to know about her. She was Norse. Pier spat on the ground in disgust, pushing air through his nose. How could he be attracted to a Norse woman?

Lars may have fallen for their witchery, but Pier vowed he would never. Disappointment in himself filled the surrounding air as he turned away. Perhaps many of his Danish kin had forgotten what treacherous, despicable people the Norse were, but Pier would not.

CHAPTER 1

"MY WORD IS FINAL, Kindra. I will not have my word questioned again," Triska said, dismissing Kindra with a wave of her hand.

"Yes, Triska," Kindra bowed, happy to be taking her leave.

The meeting with Triska had not gone well, leaving Kindra out of sorts, frustrated, and filled with anger. Kindra had been the Norse healer since before she made the trip from Norway. Her word had always been valued, and Triska had never questioned or treated her like someone beneath her before.

Kindra pulled up her hood and stormed through the settlement towards the healers' hut. She ignored people's groans in protest as she wasn't watching where she was going. Triska had been more concerned with the Danes than her own people. Kindra replayed the conversation with her leader in her mind.

"Triska, we are running low on herbs and potions. With all the wounded, I can't spare hands to go collect more. I should prioritise helping our own people," Kindra began.

"While I respect your thoughts Kindra, there are more Dane than Norse injured after this last battle. Some more gravely than others. We honour our alliance in every way. They helped defend and rebuild our home. The least we can do is heal their wounded."

"With all due respect Triska, why can't the Danes care for

themselves?" Kindra snarled, earning a sharp look from the Danish sword maidens who formed the war council.

"Enough, Kindra! My word is final. I have given you an order!"

Kindra mumbled as she pushed through a small gathering of Danish troops, ignoring the angry words they shot at her intrusion into their conversation. If the Norse could take care of themselves, Kindra had no doubt all would be well. However, Kindra couldn't fathom why Triska insisted on treating everyone as equal. Yes, the Danes had helped, but the Norse had also offered aid when the Danes needed it. And Kindra hadn't seen or heard of the Danish making the same efforts. Didn't the Danes have their own healers?

Grumbling her frustrations, Kindra almost ran into a herd of goats roaming the settlement. Then, swiftly twisting and dodging the animals, she turned around a corner and bumped face first into something hard.

Shaking herself off, she looked up to see a warrior who towered over her. She was taller than most women in the settlement, so she was amazed to see a man taller than her. Catching a better look at his face, she recognised him. He was the one staring at her during the welcome parade. She hadn't noticed where he went but noticed how he made his way through the wounded to try and reach her.

He had thick black hair pulled back with a few strands falling into his eyes, and the deepest eyes that were an almost white shade of blue. A scar stretched diagonally across his face, speaking of old battles and honour. A thick, intense nose and a short black beard framed his jaw and lips, the lips that Kindra found her eyes drawn to. Her stomach twisted like it did at sea, with excitement and fear. Her heart beat a little faster. He was the most handsome creature she had ever laid her eyes upon. She smiled at him and blushed when his eyes came down on hers.

Her attraction faded as his once gentle face filled with

wonder shifted to a look of sheer disgust and contempt. Then, snarling down at her, he barged his way past, shoving himself into her shoulder. Kindra was lost for words turning and watching as he stormed away. No man had ever looked at her that way. What had she done to offend him? Suddenly, the man embraced a brothers in arms – one of the party who travelled from the Point. A Viking. A Dane.

Kindra grumbled to herself; she swiftly left towards the healers' camp. How could she have smiled at a Dane? She kicked herself for paying him more than a moment's notice, scolding herself further the more she thought about him.

"Stupid Danes. This war needs to end so they can leave. Sooner rather than later!" Kindra said aloud, ignoring the concerned looks that stared at her as she walked.

CHAPTER 2

SHE HAD BARGED into his chest. Before she raised her head, their hands had touched for a second. It was only for a second, a gentle touch, skin on skin. So why did his hand burn with desire? Why did his hand seem to crave her touch? As he stormed away, Pier could feel her catlike eyes boring into him. He could feel her watching as he left but forced himself not to turn around and look, reminding himself she was Norse. Why was he so suddenly aware that she shared his space? Breathed the same air? Drank the same water? Shaking off the thought, Pier turned his mind to other things.

Lars had refused to leave with him and return to the Point. Their heated discussion had almost turned into blows. Replaying it in his mind was a welcome distraction from the beauty whose sweet scent of flowers and herbs still filled Pier's nose.

"Lars, you are our leader. We need you at the Point. How can you neglect your position? And for a Norse woman no less," Pier snarled.

"Speak of her in that tone again, and I shall rip out your throat!" Lars snapped back.

"Lars, see reason here...."

"Do you wish to challenge me for the leadership of our people, Pier?" Lars barked, stunning Pier into silence.

"What?....no...."

"Then know your place. I left the Point in capable hands."

"Lars! We are at war!" Pier insisted.

"Do you think I am blind, Pier? Where do you think I just returned from? The Brits are our enemy now, not the Norse. We formed an alliance. If you can't handle it, you have a choice. Challenge me for leadership or sail back to Denmark. Which will it be?" Lars demanded, standing nose to nose with Pier.

"Forgive me, Lars," Pier bowed before taking his leave.

Pier never felt called to lead. He had never wanted command of men hanging on his every word. And the truth was he knew if he did challenge Lars, he would die fighting for a position he didn't want. Yet Pier found himself questioning Lars' ability to lead. Who cared if the Norse settlement was destroyed? They should destroy the Norse and the Brits, two enemies in one swoop, showing the world who the true warriors were.

Pier was distracted by his conflicted feelings for Lars and how his skin itched from being so close to the Norse woman whose image still stung his eyes. Pier needed to get back to the Point. The open air of the settlement wasn't enough; the longer he stayed, the more he felt he couldn't breathe and might burn the whole thing down while everyone slept.

Heading to the settlement gates, Pier saw a lone horse wandering free. Already saddled, he took it as a sign from the gods. Jumping on the horse, Pier knew he had made a mistake. His first mistake was jumping on a horse that did not know him. One thing Pier liked about horses was they were loyal creatures. This horse was unknown to him, and he to it. But his biggest mistake was not checking if the saddle was secured before mounting.

Startled by a stranger on its back, the horse reared. Its saddle slid off, taking Pier with it. Pier tried to cling onto the reins, trying everything he could to stay on the horse, but it was no use. He fell to the ground with a crash, landing awkwardly on his arm. Pain shot through him, sending his vision white, and a loud snap alerted him to the severity of his injury.

Not only had he broken his arm, but a stray arrowhead missed from the clean-up of the last attack buried in the dirt sliced through his hand. The cut was long and deep, slicing through muscle and exposing bone. Pier cursed loudly at himself for making such a childish mistake.

"Are you all right?" asked a passer-by, rushing to his aid.

"He is bleeding," worried another.

"I have faced much worse than this," Pier said, shaking off his wounds as no more than a scratch.

The pain shot through him in waves, making him feel sick. It was the same sickness he had felt his first time on a ship as a young boy before he gained his sea legs. Blinking frantically, he forced his mind to stay focused lest he pass out.

"You can barely stand. Come, we shall take you to the healer," his saviour insisted.

The pair tried to reach for him, but Pier moved back. He was a proud man, never accepting help from his own, so he was even less inclined to receive aid from the Norse.

"Do not touch me, or I shall rip off your arm," Pier growled, causing the younger woman to step back.

"I would like to see you try with a mangled arm like that," snapped the older woman Pier assumed was her mother. "Stop being so proud and come with us or I shall knock you on your back and drag you there myself."

As the pain intensified and the older woman refused to back down, Pier growled and rolled his eyes. Then, admitting defeat, he agreed.

The healers' camp was a small section near the gates made up of several medium huts, all connected by a tunnel of tents. Several smaller tents had been erected surrounding the huts, and healers hurried around carrying bloodies rags and collections of herbs. Cries of pain and groans of the dying echoed all around.

Like the first morning's birds' song, it was the actual sound of battle.

"Kindra, we have another one for you. Fool tried to mount a stranger's horse without checking the saddle," chuckled the older woman.

Entering the larger tent, Pier glanced around. It was full of beds. Warriors from both sides lay side by side. Broken legs, stabs to the stomach, cracked heads, and even a man missing an eye. Pier's eyes darted around; he didn't know where to look.

"Sit him on an empty bed," came the response.

The Norse healer turned, blood dripped down her apron and covered her hands. Pier sucked in a breath, face to face with the woman he hadn't stopped thinking of. And now he knew her name.

CHAPTER 3

"SIT OVER THERE," Kindra snarled, pointing to a free bed at the back of the tent.

"I am fine. I do not need your help," the Dane replied.

His voice was like gravel and sent a shiver down Kindra's spine. But it was also a reminder that he was not one of her own. Not too happy to be treating yet another Dane, she turned, ignoring him, heading to the table at the other side of the tent, looking for herbs.

"Fine. I will see you when that wound gets infected, and I shall remove the hand for you," she inwardly smiled.

Kindra heard him moan, his frustration matching hers before she listened to the bed groan under his weight. Slowly, she ground up the seeds, oils, and herbs together. What was usually a quick blend to make, she decided to take her time and make him wait. The way he looked at her earlier that day combined with his scowl on his arrival made Kindra think he could deal with his pain alone for a few more minutes.

Kindra gathered water, thread, a needle, and some rage before finally venturing to sit next to him. The Viking guarded himself when she drew near as if her touch alone would burn him alive. Then, rolling her eyes, she snatched his arm, gaining another moment's satisfaction at the groan of pain that escaped his lips. The arm was indeed broken, but a simple enough fix. The wound on his hand was another problem entirely.

"You did well letting them bring you in. If this arm is not reset now, it will heal wrong, and you won't be able to brandish a sword again," Kindra offered, leaving him for a second to grab two sticks and some rope.

"I can fight with both hands," he replied proudly.

"Most in this camp can, but you need both arms to be able to do it," she retorted.

"I shall tend to this wound first before reseting the arm," Kindra continued, dipping a rag in some water.

"I have dealt with worse wounds than this."

"I do not doubt it. If I am not mistaken, it appears you are trying to complete your collection."

The man looked back at her, confused.

"A collection of scars? Like the one across your face? This is a pretty jiggered wound; it should match," Kindra joked, but the man didn't find her comment amusing.

He sneered in disgust before turning his face away.

"Just sew me up so I can leave. I must return to the Point."

"Pier! Someone else can go and give my report. With an arm like that, you cannot ride," Lars boomed as he entered the tent.

Word of Pier's accident had somehow reached his ears. Lars stood examining Pier shaking his head.

"Perhaps you should do your duty and go yourself instead of sending others to do your dirty work," Pier growled.

Kindra was shaken by his comment to his commander, stabbing him harder than intended as she sewed up his hand, causing him to wince and snarl at her once more. She wondered if that were the only way he would ever look at her, and if that was the case, the thought crossed her mind that she should stab him again.

Continuing to sew quietly, Kindra couldn't help but watch the exchange between Pier and his commander. Lars had become stiff and his face as hard as a rock. It was clear he was trying to control his temper, but his eyes raged at his lesser speaking to him in such a way, especially while in the company of others.

"I shall put that remark down to you hitting your head from a child's mistake, not checking a saddle. I expected more from you," Lars sneered before leaving, his fury still thick in the space he occupied only moments before.

"Do you make a habit of speaking to your commander like that? What would make one so angry?" Kindra asked, finishing sewing his would and bracing his arm to be reset.

"It matters not," Pier groaned.

Without warning, Kindra twisted his arm and pulled it straight. The arm made an audible click, and with it, a loud groan threw grit teeth from Pier. Quickly Kindra secured the sticks on either side, wrapping them tightly in rope to keep his arm straight.

"Sorry, I should have given you this to bite down on," Kindra said, holding up a short biting stick.

Without a word, Pier tried to stand, preparing to leave, not wanting to stay a moment longer. The shock and pain of having bones broken and reset in such a short period made Pier's head spin. He took a step and stopped in his tracks, blinking rapidly and breathing heavily. He reached out for something to steady him before his knees began to crumble from under him.

Kindra leapt into action, gripping him before he could crash to the floor and break his arm again. She was stronger than she looked and held him up with ease. Instinctively, Pier wrapped his arm around her to steady himself, pulling her close. They stayed for a second while Pier regained his balance.

"You need to sit," Kindra breathed, looking up at him, getting lost in his pale blue eyes.

"I am fine," he replied, but his voice was shaky.

"So you keep saying."

Kindra shivered; she hadn't been this close to him since she smashed into his chest earlier. But even then, they had barely touched. Now she found herself in his arms, and to her surprise, she liked how it felt. Neither made a move closer to the bed. Their eyes were locked. He no longer held the snarl of disgust or the wall protecting him. His mask had fallen, and his face held a softer glance – The gaze of a man mesmerized by the face staring back at him. There was no malice nor hatred, only simple undertones of something Kindra felt brewing in herself. Was it curiosity or lust?

CHAPTER 4

"Come," Kindra whispered, leading him slowly back to the bed, "You need rest."

"I will be...."

"Fine? I'm growing tired of hearing that. You may not believe me, but you have lost a fair amount of blood from that hand, making you weaker," Kindra said softly.

Pier took offence to being called weak. He was far from weak and would let a broken arm and a gash to the hand stop him from his mission. He certainly wouldn't have a Norse, especially a woman, assume such things.

"You have reset my arm. You have sealed my hand. A cup of mead and some stew will set me right," Pier protested, trying again to leave, but to his surprise, the healer was stronger than she looked.

She all but wrestled him back to the bed, turning her head to the two Viking healers who worked with her for aid, something Kindra wasn't best pleased on doing. She despised the Danes; asking for help from them was not something she was accustomed to.

Pier received an angry glower from his own people, a look that startled him. How could they side with her?

"I suggest you listen to Kindra. She is a wonderful healer, and if she thinks you need rest, you do," one of the women spoke.

Looking back, Kindra tried her best to let Pier know how smug she felt. He might not want to listen to her, but he would listen to his own people. Slowly, Pier settled back, laying on the bed, allowing Kindra to pull a blanket over him for warmth.

"I shall leave you to rest. If you need anything, let me know," Kindra said, turning and continuing to give aid to the others.

Pier watched her walk away, and only then did he see the true extent of the wounded. When he entered the tent, he had only caught a glimpse of those who resided inside. Every corner was full of wounded people. A curtain in the centre of the tent Pier had mistaken as a wall moved in the breeze revealing another room full of both Norse and Dane. Looking around, Pier only saw Kindra and three other healers, one Norse and the two Danes who had scowled at him.

The severity of the situation they found themselves in washed over Pier like a wave. Four healers were tending to at least fifty wounded, and that was just in the tent. Pier wondered how many more resided in the huts and smaller tents in the healers' camp.

These wounded were from the latest battle, a good amount of their forces out of action. Pier worried that if the British attacked again, there wouldn't be enough forces left to fight back. Kindra and the others ran from bed to bed. How were they managing to heal the sick? How many would die because there were not enough hands to fix their ailments?

As questions and scenarios played out in his mind, Pier slowly drifted. His eyes grew heavy, his body grew light until the hour grew late, and sleep took hold. But rest didn't come easy. His hand burned, the skin feeling like it was tearing again every time he moved his fingers. He tossed and turned, trying to find a position where his arm didn't throb and ache. Nothing he tried worked. The pain wouldn't allow him to sleep.

"Sleep won't come?" Kindra asked quietly, careful not to wake the other patients.

Pier looked up as she drew near, a candle in one hand lighting her way, and a strange-smelling mixture in the other. Pier kept his lips tight, shaking his head and wincing at the pain shooting through his collar bone.

"Here, drink this. It shall help you sleep and ease your pain," Kindra lifted his head, pressing the small bowl to his lips.

The liquid tasted rancid and smelled much worse. If Pier had any strength of mind, he would have spat it out, but he had never tolerated pain well and was willing to accept anything to ease his suffering.

"What happened? I didn't see this many wounded return through the gates," Pier asked.

Kindra pulled up a stool; there was a lot to tell. Her face grew sombre, and her eyes moistened as she looked over the people in the surrounding beds. She clearly cared a lot for the people in her care.

"This tent is from the latest battle at the British camp. The others are from the previous attacks. Even sending out scouts, the British eluded us and attacked us many times. They almost burned this place to the ground once before. Lars and the others came and helped rebuild," Kindra answered.

Pier scowled, turning and rolling away. His face grew angry at her words as if her words had personally offended him. The Danes and the Norse were not separated in the healers' camp. Laying side by side as they had fought. Pier had glanced at a few of the wounds of his brethren. One would never ride into battle again after losing his leg from the knee. One had lost an eye. Another fought for his life as fever took hold; those were just a few he could see.

"Why did the Danes have to be involved?" Pier grumbled.

The healer didn't answer; her face didn't move. She either didn't hear him or chose not to acknowledge his speech.

"This is not our battle to fight. We waste time and resources helping *your* people instead of fortifying our home. The Point is left defenceless while Lars insists on wasting time with that Norse woman," Pier grumbled, this time Kindra heard.

"I share no love for your kind, nor this alliance, but needs must. We have a shared enemy. The British do not care about our history or whether Norse or Danish blood runs in our veins. They want us all dead," Kindra offered.

"Huh, you do not love for my kind? Yet it is my kind who come to your aid when your people are the monsters," Pier grumbled.

"You are a daring one, Dane. Rushing to insult the people who could easily poison you as quick as helping you," Kindra said with a soft grin.

"You prove my point," Pier retorted.

"Look at me that way once more, and I shall fix it, so it is permanent. What is your grievance with the Norse?" Kendra asked.

Pier shifted in his bed, his face crumpled in discomfort. Was it the pain from his arm or the painful memories that hurt him so? Kindra sat waiting silently. Pier glanced at her briefly, realizing she had no intention of leaving until he answered her questions. Pier sighed deeply, keeping his eyes locked on the tent's ceiling.

"I was a child. No more than a boy able to walk on his own. My earliest memory is one I shall never forget – Burned in my mind, forever haunting my dreams. I ventured out into my family's field. My older sister tended to the goats. My mother helped her, my brother chopped wood, and my father was healing from battle. A Norse raiding party charged into our village. Our warriors were away sailing to new lands; we were defenceless. Women, children, and wounded. They didn't care. They took pleasure in slaughtering everyone. They made my father watch as they killed my mother and sister. He died protecting me; this scar you were so quick to mock is a constant reminder of that day."

CHAPTER 5

PIER'S STORY WAS TRAGIC. Kindra felt his pain, for it was similar to her own. Unsure of what to say, she busied herself by mixing potions and blending herbs. Kindra kept a close eye on Pier; he hadn't moved since revealing his story. Kindra wondered why he had suddenly felt the urge to share his past with her. She had never liked the Danes, but since hearing the horrors of his past, she found her heart went out to him. For a moment, she didn't see a Dane. She only saw a man still dealing with the demons of his past.

His face was stone, but his eyes moistened. Kindra could hold back no longer. An urge to share her own discretions filled her. He may be part of the people she hated, but since he had shared with her, she felt she owed him the same courtesy. Keeping her bowl and mortar in hand, she sat next to Pier, noting how he didn't flinch from her arrival this time. Crushing her herbs and using them as a focal point, she inhaled deeply. She had not spoken of her pain for such a long time.

"I feel your pain and hatred as if it is my own…. because, in truth, it is. I have struggled more than most with this alliance. I do not share love or admiration for the Danes. From what I have seen, you are just as cruel and evil as you think me and mine to be," Kindra began.

Pier turned his head to look at her; curiosity and confusion painted his face.

"My father died in battle before I was born. My mother swiftly followed, bringing me into the world. My mother's parents raised me. They were the only family I knew; they were my world. I still remember it as clear as the sun in the sky. The fields burned first, then our homes. Danes ransacked our village. My grandfather stood at the door with his axe in hand. He told my grandmother and me to run. We were forced to flee to survive. That's the last time I saw him," Kindra said, a stray tear falling and hitting her hand.

"We found a new home further up the mountains, but it was cold, and food was hard to find. My grandmother was old and frail, and I had to grow up quickly to help us survive. For years, I listened to her. Her hatred for the Danes seeped into my veins. They took everything from her. Her home, her love, and all the memories and trinkets she had to remember my mother and father. The mountains were too much for her; she died that winter. The Danes took everything from me," Kindra croaked.

She was trying not to cry, trying to hold her emotions in. But it was the first time she had spoken of it to anyone. She had been holding onto her pain, unable to grieve for so long. Reliving the memories that haunted her dreams brought up fear in her stomach. Would the British do the same?

Suddenly, she felt Pier's hand on hers. Startled, she snapped her head up to face him. Piers looked back at her, and she knew. He understood her pain. He no longer blamed her for the misdeeds of the past. Seeing the understanding and, dare she say, empathy in his eyes, she no longer held him to the mistakes of his people. He was…different? She wouldn't allow herself the thought. Once a Dane, always a Dane. Alliance or not, she couldn't get past her history. Speaking it out loud confirmed it. The Danes could not be trusted.

"I should go. There are jobs to do," Kindra whispered, breaking them out of their spell.

Pier said nothing. He felt honoured she bared her soul to him, even if he couldn't figure out why. Her story was so close to his own that he understood her hatred. Yet something about her called to him. Something said she was not like the others. Despite her hatred of the Danes, she tended to them with care and respect. She was nothing like the monsters of his dreams. Instead, she was kind, gentle, strong-minded, and a skilled healer.

How can I admire a Norse woman? Has she slipped me something? Pier thought.

Pier couldn't pull his eyes away from her. He watched her with suspicion, understanding, and admiration. So conflicted, he should have pulled away but found his conflicted feelings only made him long for her more. Watching her was peaceful – so peaceful and calming that he finally drifted off to sleep.

CHAPTER 6

WELL RESTED, Pier woke. On inspection, he found that Kindra had tended his wound while he slept, applied ointment to his aching arm, and wrapped it tightly. Pier didn't know much about herbs or their mixtures. He had no idea what Kindra had applied. But whatever it was, it did the trick. He woke with only a dull ache that he knew he could manage.

He remembered her story as he examined his hand further. Her story was just as tragic as his own. She had been left to fend for herself at such a young age, alone in the world at the hands of others. He could understand her frustration with the Danes; it mirrored his own with her people. He knew loneliness, fear, and hunger, and finding that in another was rare. She was a kindred spirit who shared pain that no one else knew. He had taken his pain and channelled it into battle. He trained to be the best warrior he could be, priding himself on bringing down the enemy no matter the cost. He carried his anger with him every day. Kindra was the opposite. She could have turned to rage. Instead, she used her anger to help others. She tended to the descendants of those who wounded her. She consoled and offered the dying respect. She was remarkable. Pier could never imagine doing such things.

Kindra was bathing and redressing a large wound on a

sword maiden's side. Pier lay still watching her at work. She offered soothing, calming words. She consoled the grieving as they prayed at the side of the dying. She rushed from patient to patient. It was a warm day, the tent only making the heat worse. Sweat pooled at her brow, strands of hair clung to her face, and she was covered in the blood of others.

The other healers were busy in the other tents and cabins, leaving Kindra alone. She stopped every once in a while for the tiniest sip of water. She looked exhausted, as though she had been up all night. Pier couldn't leave her to face this battle alone. He had been dismissive of her, snarky even. Yet she had seen past it and tended to him all the same. She was a better person than he. She had a heart of solid gold.

"What are you doing?" Kindra asked when he joined her side, collecting herbs.

"You need help," was his only reply.

"I need nothing," she answered, taking the herbs from his hands, placing them back on the table, and slipping to the next room.

Pier followed her and watched closely. He wanted to help but, in truth, didn't know where to start. A hand reached up from a cot pulling at his leg. A charred and burnt face looked back, a body so weak it could barely move. A voice, hardly a whisper, begged for water. That's when Pier knew what he needed to do. Grabbing water, he quenched the thirst. Going from bed to bed, Pier helped by making the wounded comfortable. He offered consoling words as best he could and coddled a crying child at her mother's bed.

Kindra appeared, pulling him to one side.

"What are you doing? Go back to bed," Kindra insisted.

"I cannot fight with a broken arm nor ride. So let me be of some use here," Pier said.

"You know nothing of herbs or potions," she assumed, and she was right.

"I shall not mix or give out anything you do not approve. The least I can do is comfort the disturbed, bath wounds, and anything else I can. You are overrun. You cannot do all this alone," Pier offered, finding her chose his words with much more care than usual.

"Who says I can't?" Kindra asked, folding her arms and cocking an eyebrow.

"Please, I shall go crazy doing nothing all day," Pier pleaded.

Kindra rolled her eyes and shook her head in disbelief, with an ever-so-slight grin crossing her lips. Reluctantly, she accepted. She gave him rags, water, and a small pot of the foul-smelling mixture she had offered him the night before. Then, briefly explaining how to use it and what to do, she sent him on his way. She never looked back to check on him, focusing solely on those in her care. Yet Pier found with every spare moment he had his eyes sought her out in the crowd.

The longer Pier spent in the healer's tent, the more he realised that when it boiled down to it, not everyone was as cruel as those of the past. He was still unable to let go of his hate but finding slowly, it was easing. An older Norse soldier, years past the age he should be for fighting battle, told Pier of his family. He told the story of how he met his wife, funnily enough, a Dane, and how they had kept it secret for years, passing her off as a Norse woman. Everything he did was for her and his children. His wounds were some of the worst Pier had seen. The man struggled with pain and needed rest. Pier tried to stay hopeful, but the man knew his end neared. Pier recognised a fellow warrior and wanted to make his passing as painless as possible.

"I shall be back with something to help you sleep," Pier offered softly.

The man reached up, gritting his teeth through the pain of stretching. Then, softly grabbing Pier's hand, he smiled.

"Thank you, my friend. If I do not make it, find my daughter, Estrid, and tell her that I am finally with her mother," the man said, a tear slipping from his eye.

Pier was lost for words. Pier gripped the man's hand gently, offering a nod of agreement before heading off to find Kindra.

Kindra was not in the tent, he searched a few of the smaller ones, but she was not there either. Finally, peaking inside the cabins, he came across several other healers who directed him to the drying shed.

The drying shed was a tiny wooden building by the main gate. Inside hung herbs, shelves stacked with jars of mixtures ready to be used, and at the back, hunched over a small table grinding a stone wheel, was Kindra. Looking around, Pier was alarmed. The shed was almost empty. How would they tend the sick?

"What herbs do we need? Where can I find them?" Pier asked.

Kindra cried out in shock, jumping, not realising Pier had entered.

"By the gods, do you make a habit of sneaking up on people?" Kindra gasped, her hand clutched to her chest.

"Only my enemies," Pier stopped realising his poor choice of words. "I didn't mean to startle you. I need something to help with pain and sleep. The other healers said you might be here."

Kindra rummaged through the shelves only to groan in frustration. She was out of what he needed. Pulling herbs, jars of liquid, leaves, seeds, and berries, she quickly brewed up a small batch.

"I didn't realise supplies were so low," Pier said, closing the small space between them.

A mixture of strange smells filled his nose, making his head dizzy. The smells conflicted with each other. One would make him sleepy, and the next would start his senses. He didn't want to be in the shed much longer as he grew overwhelmed.

"With the added forces and all the wounded, we ran out fast. I haven't had time to retrieve anymore yet," Kindra said, mixing her concoction with speed.

"Then allow me to help. Where can I find what we need?"

Pier asked, surprised by how often he had used the word 'we' as of late.

"We need so many, and I do not have the time to educate you on them all," Kindra sighed.

The pressure of her job was mounting day by day. Pier wanted to ease her burden. Reaching out, however, the room began to sway before his eyes. A high-pitched buzz rang in his ears, and his body grew heavy.

"Pier?" Kindra asked, jumping across the space and catching him before he fell for the second time.

Once again, Kindra wound up in Pier's arms. He relied on her to keep him steady. His body shook, his vision became hazy, and a heat spread through him he had never felt before. Sweat pooled at his brow and ran down his neck. The only thing keeping him centred was Kindra, feeling her in his embrace and her familiar scent that differed from everything else in the shed.

"Pier?" Kindra asked.

He couldn't see her clearly, just an outline of her frame bathed in white light as he blinked manically.

"You have a fever. Let me look at your hand," Kindra guided Pier back, sitting him on a chair and pulling at his arm.

"It's getting infected. Come, let's get you back into bed. I have something to fix you before infection sends you to meet your ancestors."

CHAPTER 7

PIER COULDN'T LIE; Kindra was right. He could feel sickness creeping in. His stomach flipped, his body shook, and he needed help to simply walk. Yet he wasn't so sick he couldn't notice an attractive woman when he saw one. Being so close to Kindra as she carried him back through the camp to bed, he noticed things he hadn't noticed before. She had dark rings around her irises, framing the beauty within her eyes and a small beauty mark under her right eye. With his arm around her, holding onto her, he could feel the contours of her body. He tried to avert his gaze, but it was impossible. Even with his double vision, he could see her breasts' beauty under her apron. Not too big, but just a hand-ful, exactly how he liked it.

Sitting him on the bed, she left to retrieve her potion. Pier turned his nose up at the smell, it made him wretch, but Kindra insisted he drink it. Laying him down, she soaked a rag in cold water and placed it on his forehead. Then, sitting at his side, she took her time to make sure he was okay.

The effects of the mixture took hold quickly. Warmth spread through him, and his head spun in a new way. His head felt light, leaving him feeling like he had drunk his weight in mead, a side effect loosening his tongue.

"You are a good woman, Kindra," Pier grinned, sluggishly reaching out to stroke her face.

Kindra grinned. Amused while realising what was happening, she batted his hand away softly.

"You have a good heart. I see that now. I was blinded first by your beauty, then by my pig-headed hatred. But now I see clearly," Pier slurred his words.

"Hush," Kindra laughed softly, her cheeks turning pink.

"I want to sing it from the rooftops. Once a man blinded by hate, Pier has had his eyes opened by the magical healing hands of Kindra, the Norse healer," Pier sang a little too loudly.

The other healers shushed, passing Kindra a look of annoyance.

"Hush, Pier, you will wake the others," Kindra smiled, trying not to laugh.

"You have healed me, Kindra. Not just my wounds by my mind. You are truly magnificent," Pier exclaimed.

"You are drunk from my potion. You know not of what you speak," Kindra insisted, blushing further.

"The potion may have loosened my tongue, but my words hold meaning. You are beautiful, and seeing you smile. Well, it is a smile the gods should envy," Pier grinned.

Kindra continued trying to keep Pier quiet, blushing as his compliments came thick and fast. She brushed off his hands as they wondered of their own accord.

"Since you have miraculously healed him, perhaps you could do the same for us," jibbed one of the sword maidens resting nearby.

"Or at least give him something to hold his tongue before I rip it permanently from his mouth. I am trying to sleep," groaned another.

"She is supposed to be a healing, not romancing the sick," remarked another.

Kindra tried to ignore their words, but they cut her deep. Was she neglecting her post? Had she allowed a Dane to woo her so effortlessly? How could she forget everything from her past because of a few sweet words passing lips?

"Oh, hush. I am a man free of pain and free of mind. I want to celebrate," Pier cheered.

"The maidens are right. You should rest. The potion will word faster while you sleep," Kindra said swiftly, fleeing from the tent.

CHAPTER 8

PIER DIDN'T KNOW when he fell asleep or woke; he could barely remember anything after meeting Kindra in the drying shed. One thing for sure, he was feeling much better, clean even. His fever had broken, and he felt strong again. He put it down to a combination of Kindra's herbs and a lot of rest since he could join the battle.

Looking around, he saw everyone else was asleep. A few candles still burned, offering the tent a little light. It didn't take him long to realise it was the middle of the night. Turning onto his side, he saw Kindra sleeping in a chair beside his bed. She looked peaceful, but he couldn't imagine her feeling very comfortable.

Her hair cascaded across her face. She looked peaceful for the first time in days. Pier looked at her tenderly. Slowly, his memory started to return. He had showered her with compliments, spoke of things he hadn't even had time to process himself. But even as the conversation returned, he didn't regret it; he meant every word.

He had told her how beautiful he thought she was, how her curves tantalised him. That was the last thing he spoke before she fled. He wondered if the angry words of the nearby sword maidens influenced her or if she was wary of him. Pier reached up, gently moving the hair from her face and tucking it behind her ear. His fingers brushed her cheek, and fire spread through him. How had she brought down his defences so easily? Suddenly, a thought popped into his head. If she made his body react like this with a simple brush of his fingertips, what would it feel like if she were to touch him – Not as a healer but as a woman wanting a man? He remembered how she blushed and accepted his words, not once brushing them away. She had stayed with him through the night. Did she have similar feelings?

His cock had woken with him, hard and throbbing as his mind gave way to images of her body under her dress. What would it feel like to stroke her skin with his lips? His cock begged to be touched, begged for release. Pier was all too happy to oblige. With her beauty within reach, his eyes wandered her body, fixating on her chest as it rose and fell. His hand reached between his legs; taking hold of himself, he sucked in a breath. Trying his best not to alert anyone sleeping of his actions.

Kindra hummed softly, the sound vibrating in her throat. It made Pier grow, imagining her moaning as he made love to her. Gently, Kindra snored before softly blinking herself awake. She stretched and rubbed out the kink in her neck before her eyes drifted to Pier in his moment of self-pleasure. A wicked grin crossed her lips, and her eyes twinkled. She leaned close enough for only his ears to hear.

"Stop that before you get yourself in trouble," she breathed, her breath stroking his neck, sending a shiver down his spine.

"What else can a man do when beauty such as yours is so tantalisingly within reach?" Pier asked, slipping his hand slowly up her skirt.

His fingers caressed her calf, working slowly up her thigh. Kindra didn't move to stop him, gently opening her legs wider, allowing him access to her. Pier continued to stroke himself as he played with the hair between her legs. Softly, he teased the part of her that ached the most. Leaning closer, Pier pressed his lips to her breasts as they threatened to spill out of her dress. Kindra brought his hand further, gasping as heat rose between her thighs.

It was only then that Pier remembered what had woken him. It was not a night of rest or Kindra's body next to his. A distant sound of metal, horses, stamping feet.... battle. His eyes grew wide, and he pulled himself away.

"What's wrong?" Kindra asked, startled by his sudden departure.

"Do you hear that?" Pier asked, grabbing his tunic and armour from the floor by his bed.

Kindra listened intently, her eyes widening all at once, "An attack?" she feared.

"Help me dress. I must go and fight."

"Have you lost your mind? You are in no state to fight. I need you here to help me protect the wounded and to prepare for more that may come in," Kindra snapped.

"If I do not go, there will be far more wounded to come," Pier insisted.

"And if you go, you will likely be the first to fall. Please, Pier, I need you," Kindra pleaded, glancing around at the bodies all starting to wake.

She needed him. That was all he needed to hear. Without a second thought, he nodded, and Kindra quickly helped him dress.

CHAPTER 9

IT DIDN'T TAKE LONG before the entire settlement awoke to the sounds of battle. The war drums pounded in the air, archers manned the wall, and a small gathering of warriors had been sent to guard the healers' camp. The British were angry after their defeat. They had arrived with three times the forces they had before. The wounded came in thick and fast, leaving an already overwhelmed Kindra and Pier struggling to find places to house them.

"We need to move these people. The British are destroying our forces. It won't be long before they reach us," Pier said.

Lars and Triska had assigned a small force to guard the healers' camp but the way the British cut through their troops, it wouldn't be long before they were needed in the field. Pier grew frustrated that he couldn't help, kicking himself for not checking that blasted girth strap on the saddle.

"How? If we move them, some of them won't survive. I haven't even tended to the newest patients," Kindra panicked, rushing to a fallen archer.

The woman screamed as Kindra removed several arrows from her back. She was losing blood fast; Kindra feared she wouldn't make it. This war was bringing back memories she struggled to suppress. She pushed back her tears and focused her anger on better things.

The British had come to destroy the settlement and kill every man, woman, and child in their path. Riders rode into the camp, slaying everyone in their wake. Archers rained down arrows in such force that it blocked out the moon's light. Arrows sliced through the tents wounding the sick and killing the healing. The war had arrived at the healers' camp.

"We have to cut them off before they reach here," yelled a sword maiden who entered the tent.

"Do what you can; we have it covered here," Pier reassured her.

But the maiden didn't get her chance to ride into battle. Instead, her face fell, and blood fell from her lips. Life drained from her eyes as she was sent to the halls of Valhalla. The troops had broken through the line of defences, stabbing her in the back, dropping her body to the floor like a bag of flour. The war had arrived at the healer's camp.

"I need a sword," Pier yelled, tossing a chair at the soldier who tried to rip through the tent.

"Here!" Kindra yelled, tossing him a sword.

To his surprise, Kindra had armed herself also and charged at the British, defending her patients with everything she had. She finally had a chance to slay the demons of the past, releasing all her anger on the people who threatened to repeat history.

Kindra and Pier fought, protecting the patients and forcing the British from the tent. Then, finally, seeing outside the true disaster of battle became clear. The gates of the settlement had been torn down, the drying shed was ablaze, its roof filled with flaming arrows. A line of British cavalry charged down the hill. Women and children screamed and cried, trying to flee. The dead decorated the settlement. The Vikings were falling swift and fast.

The warriors, assigned by Lars and Triska, lay scattered around the tent. There was no one there to help them. Separated from the forces, Pier and Kindra were alone, fighting with all they had to save Norse and Dane alike. Yanking an axe from the skull of one of his brothers in arms, Pier launched it across the field, giving it a new home in the face of an archer who threatened to take down Kindra.

Kindra surprised Pier the most. She was a healer, not a seasoned warrior, but she fought like a Valkyrie. The sword maidens would be proud if they could see her. A small pouch of herbs bounced on her hip. At one point, it looked like she was almost done. Her sword raised high, blocking an attack, but the Brit pushed harder, forcing her to her knees, the blade drawing closer to her face. Then, reaching into the pouch, she grabbed a handful of herbs and blew them into his face.

Startled, the man leapt back, coughing, unable to breathe. Kindra jumped to her feet, swinging her sword. She sliced his throat, kicking him in the chest and knocking him to the floor. That left only one more Brit attacking the healer's camp. Kindra and Pier faced him with all the fury of their past blazing around them. Realising he was outnumbered, the troop smiled wickedly.

"You may kill me, but I shall kill you first," he snarled.

The Brit grabbed a torch, lighting the tent's fabric as another blanket of flaming arrows filled the sky. The healer's camp began to burn. Kindra launched at the troop slicing her sword meticulously. She could have killed him quickly, but instead, she wanted him to suffer. Her cuts were enough to bring him down and weaken him but not enough to kill him.

"You shall bleed out slowly. It's a painful way to go, and I hope you suffer," Kindra snarled, twisting around and slicing at the soldier's heals, making it impossible for him to run away.

The flames spread through the tent at speed. Screams of fear and pain erupted around them. They had to move fast if they were to save anyone. The sound of a horn sang three times. The Viking sound of retreat. As the forces began to charge back inside, Pier grabbed several Vikings, enlisting their help. Kindra and others battled with the flames, and Pier ran inside. The fire raged and spread with such fury that the only option was to risk running into the flames and save whoever they could. Time was running out, and the flames grew too big to control with a few buckets of water. He returned with patients over his good shoulder as others hurried out beside him.

"Grab a wagon! Those unable to walk, load and take them to the ships. Gather what horses you can for the others," Pier barked orders, and to his surprise, not only did he like his moment in command people responded to him.

Kindra and Pier helped patients onto horseback, tossing others into the wagon, packing them as tightly as possible, sending the gravely ill to the ships, and watching them set sail. The settlement was ablaze; there was no saving it now.

"Retreat!" echoed over the battle.

"Through the forest. Head to the Point," Pier ordered.

Pier led the way, as Kindra encouraged those who wanted to give up. Armed with a bow, she scanned the woods for any impending attacks, sending her arrows flying with deadly precision. Pier knew it was an open run to the Point as long as they could make it to the hills, passed the trees, and down to the coast. They would be safe. But their journey through the woods was nightmarish. The flames appeared to chase them. Fear and terror painted the faces of everyone fleeing.

Everything the Norse had known was gone. Pier kept a close eye on Kindra; pain filled her eyes as her memory flashed back to the last time she was forced to flee her home. Pier vowed the British would suffer for making tears fall from her eyes.

CHAPTER 10

WHAT WAS LEFT of the combined forces from the Norse settlement arrived at an already heaving settlement at the Point. Word spread quickly. The Norse settlement wasn't the only one to be attacked. The settlement further up the coast had fallen too. Now, three communities were forced to group together at the Point. Luckily the Point held an old abandoned castle that the Danes had managed to rebuild. It would be a tight squeeze between the castle, ships, huts, and tents.

Pier and Kindra, with the help of the other healers, gathered the patients in the great hall and several of the surrounding rooms. Kindra watched in awe at how Pier got along with everyone. Despite the nightmare they had all endured, Pier managed to make people smile. Kindra knew he must still be in pain, but he didn't let it show if he was.

Grading respect had turned into something more. She watched as sword maidens flirted with him, their words falling on deaf ears. She remembered how it had felt to have his hands on her the moments before the battle. She remembered how when she revealed her past, he empathized with her. He was different from the men she had grown up hating. He gave openly to others, and she even heard him call her people *brother*. Finally, she could deny it any longer; she was in love.

Just as quickly as the thought warmed her heart, it sent her cold. Kindra was aware they couldn't possibly be together. Their people were working together to stop a war. What would that mean for them after that? They were from two different worlds. Pier grinned as he made his way through the great hall, but Kindra felt her heart break a little more with each step he took. She tried to flee, but Pier reached out, taking her arm.

"Kindra? What's wrong?" Pier asked.

"I....my....," Kindra stuttered.

Pier waited patiently, stroking his thumb over her skin. Kindra's eyes watched as his rough hands caressed her, comforting her enough she could speak the words.

"You once looked at me with disgust because I am Norse. I once did the same because you are a Dane. Now, everything is different. You are not like the Danes my grandmother raised me to hate, and I find myself caring for you despite everything I have ever known. But it cannot be."

Pier stepped closer, bridging the gap between them and pressing his body against hers. Looking down at her, he cupped her cheek gently, smiling as she leaned into his touch.

"I understand, more than anyone else here in the entire settlement. I was too quick to judge you. I am glad a foolish mistake led me to your arms. Perhaps we were meant to find each other. There is only one settlement on the coast now. Our people are one. We can be together and set an example for others who once shared our hate. Be the light to guide our people forward," Pier said, kissing her head gently.

"But what happens when the alliance is over?" Kindra worried.

"Kindra, do you love me?" Pier asked.

Without hesitation, Kindra nodded.

"And I love you. So let's not look past tomorrow. Let us start today. When the alliance ends, we can start a new, anywhere we want. I will follow you through sea or flame. You healed me, Kindra. Let our love for each other heal the wounds of the past," Pier whispered, finally bringing his lips to hers.

EPILOGUE

WITH THE GREAT hall acting as the new healer's camp, Lars and Triska gathered a war council in the dining hall. Scouts had reported back. The Norse settlement was destroyed. There would be no rebuilding it this time. The Point was swelling to accommodate everyone as more ships from the other Danish settlement arrived with the Jürgensen brothers and their kin.

Plans were put into motion. Lars and Triska would sail at first light to Denmark and then make their way to Norway to consult with their kings, showing a united front. Birgen and Velika were given command in their sted, Lanna and Gunnar were sent to consult with the local village, and Olga and Sten prepared to build more shelters.

"Pier, Kindra, step forward," Lars ordered.

Kneeling before their commanders, Kindra and Pier waited.

"Your bravery has not gone unnoticed. If not for you, we would have lost so much more. I hear you haven't stopped since your arrival?" Triska asked.

"That is true," Kindra answered.

"Well, spend the night in rest. The sick will still be here on the morrow. I shall make sure they are all well-tended to," Triska smiled.

All too happy to comply, Kindra and Pier took leave, heading to a small empty room at the far end of the castle overlooking the sea. They were exhausted, desperate for sleep. Climbing into the cot together, Kindra slid close, ensuring the blankets could cover them both. The sounds from the sea acted as a soothing song, bringing peace amidst all the chaos outside their door. Kindra shivered, and Pier wrapped his arms around her pulling her closer, kissing her head softly.

Kindra's eyes grew tired. She snuggled in beside Pier, her head on his chest, listening to his heart's slow, steady beat. Pier stroked her back as the sounds of crashing waves and sea birds chirping their song filled the room around them. Kindra reached over and lay her arm across his chest, ready for sleep to take her aching body. But now that their feelings had been aired, rest was the furthest thing from her mind.

Kindra grinned and slipped her hand into Pier's pants, searching for his cock. Pier rolled over onto his good elbow, his still healing arm cradled against his chest. Freeing him from his pants, Kindra carefully removed his tunic, offering an apologetic smile when he winced at moving his arm. Pier watched as Kindra rose to her feet, slipping from her dress before joining him back on the bed.

Pier rolled over, laying himself on top of her, a mountain of muscle supported on one arm. Pier had craved her touch since he realized he cared for her. A broken arm was not going to stop him. His mouth on hers was tender, soft, and gentle – A kiss of love but with every bit of passion as the flames of lust.

Kindra spread her legs and allowed him between them, guiding him through her entrance, gasping at the feel of him stretching and filling her. Pier was significant, but he entered her slowly until he filled her completely. He enjoyed the feeling of Kindra accommodating and his girth and length. Then he began to move inside her. He pulled out slowly, waited, and pushed back in. He trailed kisses down her neck and back up to her lips.

The speed was agonizing. Kindra lifted her hips to meet his thrusts; she wanted more. While lovemaking was grand, she had thought of nothing but his touch since they arrived at the Point. Pier sped up his thrusts, moving faster, harder. He thrust deeper into her, driving Kindra mad, pausing when she got too close.

He pressed harder, his breathing faster and shallow; she clawed his hips, pulling him deeper still as her moans began to fill the room. Kindra wrapped her legs around him, biting at his shoulder and clawing at his back as the heat built within her. Finally, Kindra heard him gasp and felt his tremors as his release took hold, which triggered her own. Feeling him come apart, pulsing inside her, made her clench and squeeze him tight. Pier felt her response and groaned at the magnificence that was Kindra.

Kindra spasmed around him, her back arching forcing him deeper and sending tremors shooting through her body. She had never experienced ecstasy like this before. Pier rolled onto his back, stretching out his shoulder and wiping sweat from his brow. Then, scooping his arm under her back, Pier pulled her to him, laying her over him.

Kindra reached down and smiled, finding he was still hard, still ready to receive her. Lifting up, she slid down him, gasping as he spread her wide. She rocked her hips rolling her back, her hands resting on his chest. Pier took her breasts in hand, a handful indeed as he tweaked her aching nipples as she rode him. Still writhing from the effects of their first lovemaking session, it didn't take long for them to come apart again.

Panting, sweat glistening on their skins, Kindra lay on Pier's chest, falling asleep to the steady rise and fall of his chest, the beating of his heart, and his soft kiss on her forehead.

FIRST LIGHT after a night of being somewhat well rested, Pier and Kindra stood at the dock preparing to see Lars and Triska off to sea. The settlement gathered, waiting for the words they all needed to hear to ease their quaking hearts. Lars and Triska did not disappoint.

"An alliance had been forged. We no longer stand as Norse and Dane. Together, we stand as one people. Mighty warriors with a shared enemy. We sail to our kings to show that our people have put our differences aside and come together to bring down our shared enemy," Triska's voice roared for all to hear. The crowd erupted in cheers, war cries and song.

"Our kings will see what a mighty force our people are. Look at you all. A force to be reckoned with. This land is our home. The British will not take from us again. Divided we fell but united as one, and we shall take on all of England. With the forces of our nations combined, we shall bring an army to make this island tremble at the sight of Vikings, and the British shall be the ones to fall!" Lars roared.

THE END
Did you enjoy the Pier and Kindra's story?
Please review it on Goodreads, or Bookbub.

Did you enjoy the entire box set?
Review, rate or recommend it on Goodreads and Bookbub!

Join my newsletter to stay updated on upcoming releases!

Milton Keynes UK
Ingram Content Group UK Ltd.
UKHW040832120224
437701UK00001B/80

9 781998 178001